The Ghost Files

Volume 5 (Series Finale)

By Apryl Baker

The Ghost Files

Copyright © 2017 by Apryl Baker.
All rights reserved.
Second Print Edition: August 2018

Limitless Publishing, LLC
Kailua, HI 96734
www.limitlesspublishing.com

Formatting: Limitless Publishing

ISBN-13: 978-1-64034-992-6

Dedication

For Rami Rank and Sharyn Steele

A Note From the Author

When I wrote the first book, I did the normal thing. I spit-shined it and sent it out on its own merry way into the world of agents, fully expecting, like all authors, to have an agent snap it up.

That's not what happened.

Instead, I got rejection after rejection, some going so far as to tell me that the book would never sell to any teen in the YA market. After you receive over 50 rejections telling you your book is basically crap, it puts you in the corner with a pint of ice cream, a box of tissues, and a *Supernatural* marathon running while you cry your eyes out.

I almost deleted the manuscript from my computer. That is how upset I was. Then a friend gave me the same advice I gave them. Believe in yourself, even when no one else does. They suggested I put the book up on Wattpad and see what kind of reaction I got from real readers.

So, I did, and the response was overwhelming. You guys were amazing.

I had over a million reads in less than a month. What that said to me was maybe my silly nonsense wasn't so silly after all.

I owe the success of this series to everyone at Wattpad, from the readers, to the staff at Headquarters for supporting this series and doing everything they could to make sure people knew about it. Wattpad is why I have a publishing contract for the books and why it was optioned for film. YOU, the readers, did that.

My readers are why I continued to write. If I can entertain even one of you, then all the sacrifice and sleepless days and nights are worth it. I love and appreciate everyone who takes the time out of their busy days to stop and read my work. Thank you so very much.

Mattie Louise Hathaway. She's my hero. She's also based on some foster kids I got to know whose stories horrified me. Those kids broke my heart, and I hope that reading Mattie's story, they know someone was listening. There are so many wonderful foster homes out there where children are protected and cherished, but there are just as many bad ones too. No one wants to open their eyes and admit they are there or do anything about them. So, I hope you, the reader, if you ever come across a foster home where you know they are mistreating the kids, please be like Mattie. Stand up and say something. Tell your teacher, your parents, your neighbors, a police officer, just tell someone. Don't sit there in silence thinking someone else will do it. Those kids need help, and I hope you're brave enough to help them.

I get so many emails and messages from people who tell me Mattie's story struck a chord with them, that her life is so much like their own. I get emails from foster kids who tell me Mattie gave them the courage to speak up, and that warms my heart so much. I get emails from kids who tell me Officer Dan inspired them to become a police officer when they grow up. That is amazing.

This series has done so much for so many people. Mattie has helped so many people.

But this part of her life must come to

an end, so I hope you will stick with her through the last book, the book where she'll have to make some hard choices and face things that are unimaginable.

And when we all get to the end of this chapter of her life, I want you to know it means so much to me that you stuck with us. You read every book and laughed and cried, and yelled in anger.

But most of all, I want to say THANK YOU!

I love each and every one of you.

Hugs and smooches,

~Apryl Baker

Prologue

Georgina sat at the small dresser, brushing her long sable hair. Hazel eyes twinkled at her in the mirror while she imagined the night to come. Everything she'd ever wanted would be hers. Her blood debt would be not only paid, but she'd be rewarded for finally giving him what he'd craved for over a century.

She splashed on some of her favorite perfume, Poison Girl, and then slid into the simple black dress. It hugged her curves in all the right places. Her six-inch stilettos completed her ensemble. She looked every inch as dangerous as she was.

The baby's cry wailed through the monitor beside the bed. She looked at it, annoyed. She couldn't stand the filthy urchin. Thank goodness she hadn't needed to be present for its conception or birth. The child was a means to an end, and tonight...tonight that end would pay off big time.

When the wailing got louder, she opened her bedroom door and shouted for the nanny. "Amanda!"

With what they paid the girl, you'd think she'd be quicker about her duties, but she might have a reason to shirk some of her responsibilities. Georgina's half-brother had been hanging around. The Cranes didn't know they were related. They shared the same father, but Lawrence was an illegitimate child. Her family ignored him. He amused Georgina, though, and was just as ambitious as she was. He'd taken a shine to Amanda. What did she care, as long as it didn't interfere with the girl's duties?

Where was she? Georgina stepped out into the hall, intending to shout for her again. If her brother was holding the girl up, they'd have words. Tonight had to go off without a hitch.

She heard singing. A lullaby. Curious, she walked down the hallway toward her daughter's nursery. What she saw confused her. A vision of herself sat in the rocker singing to the child. The woman sitting there loved the child. It was in her voice, her eyes.

Georgina wanted to snarl and snatch the thing out of her arms. She loathed the little creature smiling up at the copy of herself. What was happening?

"Shh."

She jumped when Silas whispered to her. The demon stood next to her, and his grin made her shudder. Silas was someone she feared, even though it was Silas who had made tonight possible. But why was he here now?

"Watch, my little Georgie girl."

The nursery door opened, and the baby's nanny came in, looking sad and anxious. The woman looked up from the rocker. "Is it time already?"

"If we are going to do this, we must do

it before he returns."

What were they talking about?

The woman stood, the baby in her arms. "Are you sure you can keep her safe?"

"Yes, I promise." Amanda nodded. "I will keep her safe no matter the cost."

Georgina watched as the woman's gaze swept around the nursery decorated in soft tones of pinks and greens. Nothing she herself would have chosen. The pain on the woman's face again pierced her heart. Why was she feeling what her lookalike was?

"Please take care of her. I've lost one child already, and to willingly give this one away is almost more than I can bear."

And then she understood. This was the child's real mother. The essence that had been housed in her own body so the girl could be conceived with all the gifts her true mother possessed. The pain she felt was a pain her body, now housing the woman who shouldn't be here, was feeling.

She turned to Silas and saw the satisfaction in his devil eyes. "You didn't really think I'd let you harm her, did you? I have my own plans for Emma Rose."

Rage overpowered her. She would not lose everything, not after all the sacrifices she'd made to get here. Silas would not stop her. She snarled and tried to hit him, but she was rooted to the spot, unable to move. The ice creeping around her held her in place while she watched her plans rot to ruin.

The woman nodded and kissed the child before handing her to Amanda. She left the nursery. Georgina blinked and found herself back in her bedroom, sitting against the bedroom door. She heard the lock slide into place on the other side.

"You did the right thing." Silas stroked her cheek.

"Why are you here?" she cried. "I made no deals with you!"

"No, my dear, but a deal was made a long time ago, and you've finally set its outcome into motion. I wish there was more I could do for you, but alas, there is not. He is going to make you beg for death."

"Please…" Deleriel *would* make her beg for death. She'd promised the girl's soul to him. That deal had now been broken, and he would make her suffer, and suffer hard.

"Shh." He put a finger to her lips. "Your part is done, and if I could, I would help you, but I cannot. Thank you for the gift you've given us this night."

And he was gone. Just like that.

No!

"Silas!" she screamed into the empty room.

The bedroom gave way to a dark cell, the walls bathed in blood, feces, and urine. The stink was so bad she turned her head and vomited. Then she noticed her hands were filthy, her hair so stringy and matted, it looked less like hair and more like a bird's nest.

Where was she? She tried to stand, but her bones hurt, and she collapsed back down on the cold dirt floor. Something scurried, and she twisted, trying to see what it was. Rats, maybe? She hated rats. They were the one thing she truly feared.

Her father had been angry and locked her in the cellar of one of their country homes once. The inhabitants enjoyed her company. Three days locked in a tiny space with rats.

A door opened, and light shone through the darkened space. Yellow eyes met hers, and she rolled, hiding from the glee in their depths. She knew those eyes. Memories flooded her mind, memories of the boy feeding from her, the pain so sharp, it could never really leave her.

"Be at ease."

Terror seized her. Deleriel. He was here to torture her again, or let his son feed from her.

"Please…no more."

"I'm not here to harm you, my sweet." He came over and helped her sit up. "How would you like to go home?"

"You'll set me free?" she whispered.

He smiled lovingly at her. "Yes, but you have to do something for me. Will you?"

She looked up into the eyes of her warden, hope flaring for the first time in fifteen years. "Whatever you want."

Chapter One

~ *Mattie* ~

Whatever you want.

The promise echoes in my mind loud enough to block out the sounds of Zeke arguing with the head of neurology. I'd told my father what happened, how the Fallen Angel Deleriel had Mary held captive, as well as Dan's little brother, Benny. I shy away from thoughts of Benny, who even now is in the hands of a monster. If I let myself think about what the kid is going through, it'll bring back memories of my own captivity and torture at the hands of my old foster mother turned serial killer, Mrs. Olson. I won't be any good to anyone if that happens.

I need out of this hospital.

Deleriel wants me alive, so he did his Angel thing. My seizures have stopped, and my brain has been miraculously healed. I told Zeke about that too. He understands why I need out. The doctor can't explain my scans, so he's arguing about releasing me before he runs more tests, but the longer I'm here, the longer Benny is in the hands of the man who has butchered countless children.

Dan and Eli left the minute they got me back to my room. I called Zeke, who wasn't that far away. He'd been at dinner with his parents. I hadn't gone into details over the phone, but urged him to get his butt back here sooner than humanly possible. It was minutes before he came bursting through the door, terrified, only to find me calmly staring out the window at the parking lot below.

That had been last night and several head CTs later.

"Look, you can either sign the

discharge papers, or I'm leaving anyway." Enough is enough. I have more important things to do than stand here listening to them bicker. To make my point, I take my clothes out of the little closet and go into the bathroom to change.

I try not to notice the maze of bruises that decorate my body. Battle wounds. Deleriel hadn't seen his way clear to heal those, only the life-threatening brain injury. I'm sore all over, but that's a testament to my will to survive. I learned a long time ago, if you don't fight, you die. Hit first, before you can get hurt. It rings true now more than ever. Deleriel made a mistake taking my sister and Dan's brother. He will suffer for it.

Even if I have to make a deal with Silas to do it.

Silas hadn't told me what he wanted in return for his help, but I'm guessing the price is going to be my soul. I won't think twice about giving it up if it saves my sister and an innocent child. Besides, I deserve this. Everyone who cares about me always ends up hurt, their lives destroyed. Because of me. They may not blame me, but I am at fault. If this is my punishment, I will take it.

But first I have to get out of this danged hospital.

The doctor's gone when I come out, and Zeke is staring out the window, tired and worried. I can't blame him. I've put him through a lot. He only just found me, and I think I've aged him in the few short weeks I've known him. Yet another instance of me ruining the people who love me.

"Doctor finally give up?" I grab my shoes and sit down to pull them on.

"Yes." Zeke turns toward me. I can see him out of the corner of my eye while I tie my shoelaces. "I'm not sure he's wrong, Mattie. I think we should run more tests, just to make sure."

"I'm fine." I wave off his worry. "Deleriel is an Angel. Maybe a bad one, but still an Angel. He said himself he couldn't have me die before I gave him my soul." I don't say what we both are thinking. I must have been close to death for him to completely heal me. I might not have survived another seizure.

For that much, I am grateful. I don't want to die. I haven't survived a serial killer, crazed ghosts, a psycho, and creepy demon children only to fall victim to brain seizures. How fair would that be?

"I don't think so." He comes to stand by me, his hand on my shoulder. "Medical issues aside, you're in the crosshairs of a Fallen Angel. 'Fine' is not the word I'd use to describe it."

"I'll give you that." I flash him a weary smile. "I'm a tough cookie, Zeke. It's going to take more than a Fallen Angel to take me down."

"I almost believe you."

My dad's pretty awesome. Sure, he's a criminal and on the FBI's most wanted list, even though they can't make any charges stick, but he's still a great dad. Instead of arguing with me, he just accepts the fact that I do what I have to do. Maybe because he does what he has to do, even if it causes him to commit crimes sometimes. I'm not judging, since he's never judged me. Not once.

All in all, it takes another thirty

minutes for discharge papers to be issued and for the nurse to go over signs and symptoms I need to watch out for. Don't think it's going to be an issue, unless one of those creepy, yellow-eyed, demonic kids touches me again. That's what caused the seizures to start in the first place. My human body can't handle some of my reaping abilities. Abilities only a full-grown reaper should have.

Kane, my…reaping trainer…best phrase I can come up with, warned me that every time one of the dead touches me to show me what they can't say, it makes my reaping abilities surge up to sort it out, and my very human brain can't handle it. It seizes. Maybe Silas will know of something that can help stop that. But at what price? With a demon, there's a price for everything.

Zeke is driving the same car he loaned to Dan the other day. The day he kissed me and confused everything. I'd made myself give up on Dan and let Eli in, but then he went and kissed me. Just one more thing on top of an already insurmountable pile of crap to deal with.

Buckling the seatbelt, I notice something on the back floorboard…a book. Holy crow, it's one of the books Heather gave me. She said they'd help me understand my reaping heritage. Maybe there's something in there about how to protect myself from the souls who unknowingly hurt me.

Zeke looks curiously at me when I lean back and pick them up. "What are those?"

"Eli's mom loaned them to me. She's their Historian. The Malone family has always been tasked with watching over living reapers. These books are about that."

"Hmmm." He puts the car in gear and backs up. "How do I not know this?"

"Have you ever let anyone know you're a living reaper?"

"No." He cuts off the AC, shivering. "Papa is forever turning the AC on. He doesn't understand how cold we are."

"They don't share our abilities?"

Zeke yawns. "The ability was passed down from my father's side, but no, Papa is not a reaper. To gain our abilities, you

18

must technically die. Papa is as healthy as a horse."

"Then how did you become a reaper? Was it an accident, or did you…?" I stop, realizing what I am asking. It might not be a good thing to ask him.

"Or did I purposefully try to kill myself to gain more power?" He chuckles. "It's a fair question, given what you know about me. I didn't do it on purpose, but I might have if I hadn't drowned first."

"You drowned?" My own near drowning teases at the edge of my memories, but I resolutely refuse to remember the ghost girls who wanted me dead. One had almost succeeded in drowning me.

"I was seven. There was a blackout, and our generator hadn't been replaced in years, so Mama turned off the AC to make sure we didn't drain the generator. It was sticky hot, and I felt like I was suffocating. I remember that. So, I did the one thing I'd been forbidden to do. I went swimming without telling anyone. Not the brightest idea, but I was only seven.

My leg cramped up, and I couldn't get out. Papa found me face down in the pool. I'm not sure how long I was dead, but he was able to revive me. They rushed me to the hospital, and that's where I had my first encounter with a ghost."

"Was it scary?"

"No, but then I didn't really understand what was going on. It was a girl. About twelve. We learned later her parents had starved her to death. She kept trying to talk to everyone, but no one answered her. I told her I could hear her, and she turned to me, shocked. Mama asked me who I was talking to, and I told her. Scared Papa half to death. That's when he told me about living reapers."

"Were you able to help her?" That is so sad. My first ghost had been an old man who didn't know he was dead.

Zeke shook his head and took the exit that would lead us back to his apartment. "No. They sent me home, and I never saw her again. But I saw others, ones that terrified me. I spent the first two years screaming every night when a new horror appeared. Papa called in specialists to help, people who knew how to protect me." He held up his wrist, which had some kind of bracelet on it. "Iron. They don't touch me anymore, but they still come around when I'm not at home. Can't salt the doors and windows everywhere you go."

"I ignored them, and they eventually went away. It was my mantra, ignore them and they'll go away. At least until Sally died."

"Sally?"

"My foster sister from Mrs. Olson's. I saw her ghost, and that's what sent me down the rabbit hole trying to find her. I met Dan, who was the only person who believed she wasn't a runaway. He was the first person to ever believe in me."

"You and Daniel are very close, aren't you?"

A small smile tilts my lips. "Yeah. He always tells me he's in it for the long haul. No matter what I did to push him away, he was always there, steadfast and ready to help me. I even got him busted for breaking and entering once. Did I tell you about that?"

"You convinced a police officer to break into a building?"

"Yup. Then he tried to explain to the cops what we were doing in a dead person's house. Poor guy. He can't lie. I stepped in and told this sob story the officer bought hook, line, and sinker. I think that's the day Dan Richards realized exactly how scary I can be, and he *still* stuck by me."

"Would I sound like a horrible father if I admit how proud I am that you're a capable liar?" Zeke winks at me, and I laugh.

"No, but then again, we're not like most fathers and daughters, are we?"

We sit quietly for a while. Zeke is a born liar, and so am I. My rap sheet is a testament of that. I don't want to end up in jail, but it won't stop me from doing what needs to be done to protect myself or those I care about. I get that same vibe from Zeke. We're more alike than I'd thought.

"Did anyone find my phone?" I really need to talk to Dan or Eli. Benny might not have been taken by Deleriel's human vessel. It could be he's just lost, at a friend's, or even snatched by the run-of-the-mill pedophile. Surely, Deleriel wouldn't be stupid enough to take the child of the person who's hunting him?

Maybe. He might be trying to make a statement about the cop's inability to do anything to stop him. Or he could just find it funny in a sick and twisty kind of way.

"Your phone, *ma petite*?"

"It was in my purse at…at the ball."

"No, no one has returned it to me. I will call about it as soon as we're home. Is it under Mrs. Cross's plan?"

"Nah. Dan got it for me for my birthday. He pays the bill. I tried to give it back, but he refused." In fact, I'd actually thrown it at his head, pissed off about him and Meg, but he'd given it to me later, saying I needed it.

"That was nice of him."

"More out of desperation for my safety, I think. None of my foster parents would pay a cell phone bill, and I couldn't keep enough money to buy minutes on a prepaid, so I was basically without a phone. He was worried I'd get in a situation and have no way to call for help, so knowing all that, he bought me a phone and put it on his plan."

Instead of saying anything, Zeke turns down a road that will take us back to the interstate. "Where are we going?"

"The Apple Store."

"Why?"

"Because I'm guessing your phone is long gone, and Daniel is right about one thing. You need a phone."

"You don't have to buy me a new phone. They probably have mine in lost and found or something."

Two hours and several arguments later, we're walking into the apartment with a bag that houses a new iPhone, iPad, and a Mac Book Pro. Despite the fact I have a laptop, Zeke said he wanted my devices to sync up. Why in God's name he decided I needed a tablet as well as a laptop is beyond me. I was perfectly content to not buy any of it, but there was no stopping the man.

Rich people. I don't know if I can ever

have the mentality of always buying the best of everything, even if what you already have is perfectly fine. One more thing to remind me I'm not like Zeke or my grandparents. I'm just plain and simple Mattie Hathaway, trying to come to terms with a family that comes from old money. Something I don't think will ever happen.

My grandparents are waiting for us. Lila and Josiah Crane rushed up here to meet me after my near-death experience at the hands of my ex-boyfriend's psychotic brother. They are fiercely protective, and as much as that makes me all warm and fuzzy, it's also annoying. I grew up fending for myself, and I still do. They only get in the way.

I should feel horrible thinking that, but I don't. I'm a foster kid. It's who I am. I'm tough, can fend for myself, and I don't trust people. My grandparents are nice, but I don't trust them completely yet. Zeke, I do. Not sure why, but it is what it is.

"She's fine, you're sure?" Lila asks, hugging me then thrusting me back to search my eyes. "What is going on?"

"I'm fine. I promise." I gently disentangle myself. "I just need a shower, and then I have calls to make. Zeke will fill you in on everything." Before anyone can argue, I make a quick exit toward the stairs, needing to call Dan or Eli.

Since my room has no furniture yet, I head for the guest room Dan used. I take out my shiny new phone and punch in Dan's number. It goes straight to voicemail. He wouldn't have recognized the number. I leave him a message. I do the same with Mary's mom. I don't have Eli's number memorized, so I can't call him.

Falling on the bed, I take a minute to let all the events of the last twenty-four hours settle. I can hold out hope that Benny isn't in the hands of Deleriel's vessel, but the same can't be said of Mary. She's being held hostage.

I know what's going through her head. It's the same thing that's going through mine. Mary was held for weeks, whereas I was only a victim for a few days. Mary went through a heck of lot more than I did. If merely the thought of being trapped sets off a panic attack in me, it has to completely destroy her.

Please, God, help me find her and Benny. Keep them safe.

It's all I can do until someone calls me back. Pray and hope.

Chapter Two

Waiting was never my thing. I'm impatient. It gets me in trouble, but I don't care. Sitting here doing nothing is only causing my panic to rise. I'm driving myself nuts thinking about Mary being held captive, and Benny...nope, not going there.

There is one other number I know by heart, and I call it, hesitant, but I need all the help I can get.

"Hello?"

Dr. Lawrence Olivet, spook doctor extraordinaire. He sounds sleepy. Not that I can blame him. It's early, only a little after nine in the morning.

"Hey, Doc. It's Mattie. I got a new phone."

"Mattie?" The sleep flees from his voice. "Are you okay?"

"Peachy." Taking a deep breath, I ignore my instincts not to trust him and plow ahead. "Dan hasn't called, has he?"

"No. Something *is* wrong, then?"

"Yeah, something's wrong." I stop pacing and curl up in the chair, tucking my knees under my chin. "Deleriel has both Mary and Benny, Dan's baby brother."

Doc lets out what I can only assume are curse words in a variety of languages. I never would have guessed he had it in him. "When did this happen?"

"Deleriel came to me in the hospital last night and showed me Mary in a prison. She can't handle being locked up. It'll bring back every horrible memory she has of being held captive. I have to get her back, Doc."

"Slow down, Mattie. Why were you at the hospital? Did Dan relapse?"

Of course, he wouldn't know. Dan knows I don't trust him anymore and respects my decisions. Well, mostly. He has a different opinion when it comes to Doc. Not that he's wrong, but I hate liars, and the Doc lied to me from day one.

"Nope. I was in the hospital for seizures. Deleriel healed me. Can't get what he wants from me if I'm dead."

"And what does he want?"

I hear more than curiosity in the Doc's voice. There's something there I can't place, and it holds my tongue still. "I don't know, but I'm betting whatever it is, it's not good."

Doc lets out a sigh. "Don't worry, Mattie. We're going to figure this out. I already had my team overnight me books I thought we'd need. There are a few more that may help. I'll have them by tomorrow. Everything is going to be fine."

He sounds disappointed. He wants to know why Deleriel kept me alive. I don't think it's about helping me either. It's that *something* in his voice I can't place. I don't care what Dan says. Doc may have tried to help us in the past, but I'm betting he wants something from me too.

Something every bit as nefarious as Silas or Deleriel.

Or, all my years in foster care made me so paranoid, I can't tell who's trying to help me and who wants only what I can give them. Either way, I'm not trusting him with the entire truth. At least not yet.

"I can come by the Crosses'…"

"I'm not there. I'm staying with my dad. I think he can protect me better than Mrs. Cross. Besides, they don't need me dragging any more supernatural crap into their lives. I think I've done enough of that to last a lifetime."

"None of that is your fault."

So they all tell me. But it is true. I am the center of the storm, and everyone around me gets knocked down by gale force winds. Collateral damage. No one is making me believe otherwise, not even Dan. At least the Cranes are better equipped to handle the storm.

"Sure." I take a deep breath. "Read through what you have and meet me here at my dad's. Zeke might be able to help figure this out."

"You told him?" He's flabbergasted.

"Well, yeah. He's a living reaper too, Doc. He knows more about being one and the supernatural than I do. I trust him."

"Don't ever trust him, Mattie." This time Doc sounds ominous. "There are things about Ezekiel Crane you don't know. Things I hope you never know. He's…"

"A bad man." Everyone keeps telling me this. No one has to remind me of it. I sense it in him, but not when it comes to me. "Zeke is probably the only person I trust not to hurt me."

"You don't know that, Mattie."

"But I do. My dad can't lie to me. It's a gift of his I inherited. Now that I know about it and how to use it, no one will ever be able to lie to me again."

Doc goes quiet. I guess he's wondering if I'm gonna use that particular ability on him. You bet I am. I'm getting to the bottom of his agenda.

"You asked your father about his intentions?"

"Yeah. He told me all about the Oracle's prediction. He was going to do it too. Murder me and take my gifts. But once he held me, he couldn't. He loves me, Doc. I don't think there's a force on this plane or any other that could make him harm me."

"I hope you're right."

Me too.

"Call me before you come over. Maybe Dan will be here by then too. Gotta go, Doc. Talk to you later."

I hang up before he can say anything else. Bad habit Dan picked up from James, and I picked up from him, but I really don't want to get into everything pertaining to my relationship with my father with Doc. Probably not a good idea. I will need to warn Zeke about Doc and his suspicions. That is not going to be a pleasant conversation.

Seeing the books I'd deposited on the bed, I decide to read through them. I might as well, while I wait for Dan or Eli to call me back. It will at least keep my mind off everything. Hopefully.

Heaving myself out of the chair, I walk over to the bed and sit down. The smell of Dan's aftershave still lingers. I'd subconsciously chosen his room out of all the guest rooms. I guess I need to be close to him. We're connected, and I have this sense of unease and dread in the pit of my stomach. He's scared. I feel it like it's me right there, terrified and angry there's nothing I can do.

Shaking my head, I open the first book. Latin.

Dang it. I can't read Latin. You would think Eli's mom might have mentioned that yesterday. Maybe Zeke and his fancy upbringing also taught him Latin. Gathering the books together, I head back downstairs. He's in the library with Lila and Josiah.

"Mattie, shouldn't you be resting?" The worry behind Josiah's words stops me from snarking back. Something I tend to do when I'm freaked out.

"Has anyone called and checked on the investigation? No one knows my new number and I need to get in touch with Mrs. C so I can find out what's happening with Mary. Dan and Eli aren't returning my calls..."

The look on Zeke's face stops me.

What is that look about?

"Emma Rose." Zeke comes over and pulls me in his arms. "Eli is having a hard time right now."

"What do you mean?"

"Dan called me and asked me to keep you away from the Malones right now."

"Why would he do that?" My gut twists. Why do I ask questions I don't want to know the answer to?

"He needs to blame someone."

"And he blames me." Of course, he does. He's not wrong either. If I hadn't gone to New Orleans, I wouldn't have met him, I wouldn't have brought a vengeful Fallen Angel into their lives. Benny would be home safe and sound instead of in the hands of a crazed, demon-possessed pedophile.

"None of that, Mathilda Crane." Lila pulls me out of Zeke's arms. "This is not your fault. I know you think it is, but it's not. James Malone would have come here with or without your help. He investigates cases like this, and his team would have led him here eventually."

She's trying to explain it away with

logic, just as I had Meg's death to Dan. If he'd died, yes, she wouldn't have died that night, but her death wasn't one of pain and humiliation. He spared her that. He believed it because he needed to believe it. Not sure I was right or wrong, but it gave him strength. Unfortunately for Lila, my own tricks won't work on me.

"And if all else fails, my darling, remember this. You are a Crane. We take responsibility for our actions. If you feel this is your fault and can't be persuaded otherwise, then take responsibility for it and move on. Accept it, and then fix what you can."

Now, that makes more sense to me. I am to blame, and I will do what I have to in order to fix it. No matter the cost.

"There's that fire in your eyes I saw when I met you." Lila smiles and kisses my cheek. "We'll fix this. I promise."

I don't think I'll ever fix my relationship with Eli. He can't get past the fact I'm part demon. That's a truth I can't un-tell, but if I can save his little brother, that might go a long way toward at least being friends again. I'd miss having him around.

"What about Mary?" My sister is at the front of my thoughts, overshadowing even my fear for Benny. I know what she's going through. "Has anyone heard anything or know where he's keeping her?"

Josiah sighs. "Given what Zeke told us, I'm afraid he might have taken back to his lair already."

"His lair?"

"In Hell." Josiah sips at the glass of amber liquid he's holding. "I think he whisked her to the one place none of us can go."

"But isn't it just another plane of existence?" Zeke told me his family can navigate all planes. It's what kept them from being caught by authorities.

"Yes, that's true," Josiah agrees, "but there are certain places even we can't go. Hell just happens to be one of those places."

Well, fudgepops. What the heck are we going to do now?

"I've called in favors, Mattie." Josiah

does his best to assure me, but I have this sinking feeling in the pit of my stomach. No one's going to be able to save Mary. I can't lose my sister. I can't.

"Hush now, *ma petite*." It's Zeke's turn. "We'll get her back. No one's giving up. I promise."

"I have something that might help." I push away from Zeke, needing my space. I can't cry. Not now. As much as I want to, I know it won't do me or Mary one bit of good. "These are the books Heather loaned me. They're in Latin, though."

"And you don't speak it?" Zeke nods. "Neither do I, much to my parent's shame, but Papa does. Perhaps he could translate for you?"

"Of course."

I hand him the books, and he looks over them carefully. "These are ancient texts, but bespelled."

How the heck does he know that?

"The technique is as old as the Historians themselves. It's the only true way to preserve what was actually written. Things tend to change in the translations. Meanings get lost, and then the words themselves are no better than bedtime stories. This way, however, everything is preserved exactly as the author wished it to be, and the truth is forever immortalized."

Okay.

"Now, then, why don't we have your staff bring us a bite of breakfast? I can hear our girl's belly complaining as loudly as mine, and we'll read through these. We might learn a few things ourselves."

My stomach might appreciate it, but my mind doesn't. I just want answers. But I suppose eating some pancakes might calm me.

Especially Mrs. Banks' homemade ones.

Chapter Three

7 July, 1539

My name is Sylvia Fields, daughter of Stefan Larwood, Duke of Heshire. I was born and raised in London where my parents were murdered by unnatural forces, things I could not explain as a child. The Church took me in and trained me to be a Historian. They gave me the education I required to understand what happened to my parents and the tools to protect myself and my country from those same unnatural forces.

Today is the seventh day of the

seventh month in the year of our Lord 1539. It is also the day I take over the role of Historian from Lady Ana of Sussex. She gave her life to protect others, and I can only hope my life will be as worthwhile as hers and that I die in service to God as she did.

My first journal entry is something that I witnessed a few weeks ago and have tried to research, but have had no good fortune. I thought the girl insane at first, but then I witnessed what she could do. She speaks to the dead. Truly an unholy gift. Surely, this ability is not from God, but from the devil himself. Is it witchcraft or some other dark secret? I have a mind to take this to the Church myself, but before I bring anything to them, I want my research done and my facts infallible. I do not wish to embarrass the Bishop who trusted me with this post.

The girl's name is Donna O'Malley. I discovered her in a small hamlet near

Ballymote. Her father works as the castle blacksmith, and her mother died when she was but a babe. The girl is only nine. It upsets me to have to harm a child, but if I must, I will. Depravity is depravity, no matter the physical form.

Before I act, I will understand this child's ability and determine if it truly is a curse. To commit the murder of an innocent is a treason against God himself. I must be certain of my convictions. I will speak to the girl and those nearest to her before I decide what is to be done.

12 July, 1539

The child is a happy one. Her father a good man, from all accounts. She has caused no harm to any in her hamlet. None speaks ill of her or her family. But none seems to know of her affliction, as I have come to think of it. To commune with the dead is the darkest of arts and it is an affliction upon the innocence of the girl's soul. I have spoken with the parish priest, Father Galen. He knew of what I spoke, and it has troubled him as well. He sees no malice or evil in the girl. She says she helps the dead understand they are no more of this earth, and the souls she sees move on when they come to understand their plight.

Father Galen worries that it is not innocent souls she speaks with, but demons sent here to trick her into giving them all the good within her. I cannot say which of the two are right.

I spent the day with Donna. She took me to the small cemetery out by the castle. She knows I doubt her gifts. Even at such an early age, she is wise beyond her years. I see the wisdom glowing like a beacon of light out of her brown eyes. She only smiled when I asked her how she came to be able to speak with the dead. It wasn't until we were walking up the path that led behind the small church to the cemetery that she confessed to always having been able to see them. She considers them her friends, her companions. They aid her, keep her safe, and give her the knowledge she needs to help save others. Hearing such a small girl talk as if she is a woman grown unnerved me.

When we reached the church, I expected us to go into the small cemetery, but she kept walking. I was confused, as she claimed that is where we were to go, but I followed her out of curiosity. We walked deeper into the woods and came upon a clearing. Several graves were laid out before us, each marked only by a simple wooden cross. Some were weathered with age, but two looked newer than the others. Was this some sort of family burial ground?

No, she told me. It is the graves of those marked as damned souls. Donna sat down, her legs tucked under her beside the one on the very outer edge of them, the newest one. The woman buried in it was called Margaret. She was the miller's first wife. She took her own life and thus committed an act against God. The Church could not allow her on consecrated ground for such a blasphemous sin.

Margaret spoke at great length with the child, or so Donna claims. The girl is adamant that the woman did not take her own life. She says her husband murdered her so he could wed another. You see, Margaret was barren, and could not give her husband children as was her wifely duty. Those are the exact words the girl repeated to me. A child of seven should have no knowledge of the marriage bed, but Donna spoke as if she were an adult explaining it to me.

And that gives me pause. Who is putting these thoughts in her head? Is it someone in the village, or is the ghost of the miller's dead wife truly speaking to her? Or is it some unholy force, as the priest suspects? These are the things I must determine. And soon.

29 July, 1539

Today was the hardest day yet. I met a man who claimed to be a Knight of the Church. He came to protect the little girl. He claims his family has been tasked with guardianship over those with the child's gifts. Living Angels who reap the souls who need to pass on from this life to the next. I am not sure I quite believe him. He speaks of belonging to the Knights Templar. The Church declared them heretics and slaughtered them. Why would he tell me, an agent of the Church, that he is a part of an organization that has been outlawed and proclaimed an enemy of the Church?

He speaks with such conviction that I am torn. His purpose appears to be a holy one. I see it in his eyes. It is whispered that the Knights were feared because they were spawned from Angels, which our Lord has condemned in his own teachings. I do not know what to believe.

The girl has no evil in her soul. She is kind and innocent, but she sees and speaks with the dead. I spoke with a few of the village wives about the miller's dead wife. They did not wish to speak of it, but when I told them I was there from the Church to investigate her death, their tongues loosened. It would appear her husband's displeasure with her was well known, and he took another wife within only a few days of her death. A girl of only fifteen who bore him a son within their first year of marriage. She confessed her worries to a few of the other wives. He'd made veiled threats against her in the presence of others, and she feared for her life. They found her hanging from a tree a few weeks later. The church accepted her husband's word she had taken her own life.

I am no longer convinced of that. Perhaps her ghost has clung to this world in hopes of finding some brand of justice. I am not sure. The longer I spend with Donna, the more convinced I am she speaks truly. She does, in fact, hear the whispers of the dead. There was a village woman who died in childbirth three days past. I was with Donna today when the shade visited the child. The room grew unbearably cold. I sensed a threat. The spirit was angry. Donna explained to me the woman didn't understand she had died and needed to leave. The girl sat there for two hours, speaking with someone I could not see, but I felt it. It was the strangest feeling, disturbing.

The room changed. It became less hostile. Warmth chased away the cold. I asked her what had happened. She simply said she has gone from this world. The child helped the spirit understand her place was no longer among the living, but with those in God's realm. It gave me many things to think upon.

Between the child and the Knight, I am confused and frightened. What if this is a gift from our Lord? Or perhaps it is a curse disguised in the trappings of a gift. I must reach out and seek guidance.

10 August, 1539

The Knights name, as I discovered, is Heron Melavone, Duke of Caterly. I left the village shortly after our talk and travelled to our Sept House. Bishop Whitmore was there, and I put the questions I have before him. He listened intently to my concerns, and then sent me to clean up and get a night's rest. He would look into it and promised to speak of it upon the morrow.

I awoke this morn to find the Bishop gone with several of our members. Our soldiers were given orders to keep me at the Sept. I was not to leave for any reason. I became even more frightened. Had I put the child in danger by seeking counsel? And Heron? Had I condemned him to death by revealing all he'd told me in confidence? These questions plague me as I write this down.

What have I done?

23 August, 1539

The Bishop and his men returned this morn. There was an air of solemnity about them as they rode through the gates. The men looked haggard, as if an illness had taken hold. Knowing what I know now, perhaps it had. One cannot do what they have done and walk away with no scars.

The Bishop ordered the entire hamlet killed. These men carried out those orders. The child, he said, infected them all with her dark curse. The only way to save their souls was to purge them with fire. They collected every man, woman, child, and babe. Took them to the Church and burned them all. All except for the priest. He returned with them, but I have not seen him. I've heard the screams, though.

Bishop Whitmore assured me his pain is necessary. Father Galen is a man of God and far less susceptible to the ways of the wicked, but any uncleanliness must be accounted for. I can only imagine what they are doing to the Father. Fire. That is the surest way to cleanse the soul.

Donna was not an evil child. She was sweet, innocent. I feel it in my bones. What happened to that little girl and her village is wrong, but who am I to question the Church or God's will? I am but a servant of our Lord, following his teachings and guided by his learned scholar, Bishop Whitmore.

But I cannot reconcile my heart with

what my mind tells me. This act was not what the God I know would have wanted. Perhaps my own childhood experience has blinded me to the truth. Perhaps the Church is wrong in how it deals with the things it does not understand.

My heart is heavy this night. I have been taught to never question the Church or its interpretation of the will of our Lord. But I am.

Where does that leave me and my role as one of its servants fighting against the darkness sweeping through our lands?

I do not know.

30 September, 1539

The Bishop sensed my unease and has kept me with him these last few weeks. He has guided me in prayer, and I think he is finally convinced I am able to take up my role again. Father Galen requested to join me on my travels, and

Bishop Whitmore agreed. It disturbed me, this quick agreement. Father Galen was cleansed, has been performing his duties here at the Sept, but his eyes are as haunted as his flesh is scarred.

They cleansed him in fire as I had suspected. His body is disfigured, even his face having not escaped the wrath of the Bishop. When I was allowed to see him, I feared he would not survive. Fever had taken hold. The Bishop assured me it would be fine. The fever was the fight for his soul. If he lived, he won the battle and his purity in God restored, and if he died, then he could not combat the evil inflicted upon his soul.

Father Galen has been quiet since the cleansing. He speaks rarely and moves quietly. At times, I wonder if his mind has suffered. He is not the Father Galen I knew. His body survived, but his spirit is broken. Yet one more reason I question our methods. Father Galen was no more infected than I, but yet he was cleansed simply because he was there.

He did ask to join me on my travels, so hopefully there may be something left of the man I knew. We shall see.

We leave on the morrow. I will be glad to get away from the Sept and its watchful eyes. To get out and do God's work, fight the evil I find.

I will be more cautious in my counsel this time. I will not have another village burned because of something I do not understand.

Chapter Four

We are all quiet when Josiah stops reading and closes the book. I always knew the Church had a dark past, but I never really understood how dark. I had no idea stuff like that really happened. I mean, you see it in movies, but to imagine that happening to someone in real life? Just...wow.

I'm pretty sure these types of journals are kept as far away from the public as possible. The Church has worked hard to clean up its public image. They condemn these things in the modern era.

"I think we all need a break." Josiah sets the book down and turns to Lila, who's a little white. "Why don't we go out on the balcony for a bit of air, sweetheart?"

Lila nods and lets Josiah lead her out of the room.

"Forgive my mother. Her sister was burned by witch hunters."

"Zeke, you're seriously telling me there are still witch hunters today?" I can accept people who knew no better did it, but in today's world? Mind. Blown.

He purses his lips. "Sadly, there are still a great many dangers left over from an archaic age."

"Will you tell me about it? I mean, if it's not…"

"Of course, I'll tell you, *ma petite*. It's something you should know anyway. You must be prepared."

Prepared for what, exactly?

"Mama's sister, Madeline, was only seventeen when she died. She made the mistake of trusting someone she shouldn't have. This happened outside of London, in my grandparents' country house. Mama's parents had gone into the city for the week, and the girls stayed home. Mama said she wasn't well. Something about her stomach. The hunters came in the middle of the night. Madeline made Mama hide and faced them alone. They declared her a witch and quoted the Bible. 'Thou shalt not suffer a witch to live.' That's all Mama heard. The hiding spot my grandparents built was very good. Thankfully, she wasn't able to hear her sister's screams. She stayed in that spot until her father found her two days later. They'd killed everyone in the house just for being there and burned her sister at the proverbial stake. Right in front of the house for all to see. I'm surprised they didn't burn the house down."

"That's awful." I understand Lila's reaction now. The journal Josiah just read from mimicked her sister's death in so many ways. The trauma she must have suffered, knowing she lived when everyone didn't. "Did they find out who did it?"

"Of course and they paid for their crimes." The warning not to ask any more questions is clear. Not that I want to, anyway. I have an idea of what happened. What little I know about my family pretty much says those who did that suffered horrible deaths. And in this instance? I can't say I would have done any different. The police can't always serve justice, and even when they do, sometimes it's no real justice at all.

"You must always be vigilant. Our family, both the Cranes and Duchanes, have delved into the supernatural for as long as we've existed. Because of that, we'll be a target for those zealots for an eternity. If you take nothing away from today, know this one simple truth—trust no one outside your family."

"I trust Dan."

Zeke smiles and hugs me. "Yes, Emma Rose, you can trust Daniel. He's family, though. The boy's proven it enough times."

"Do you think you'll ever remember to call me Mattie?"

"I do try, *ma petite*. You have been Emma Rose to me since the day you were born, and I guess you'll always be my Emma Rose."

"I've been thinking about that." I disentangle myself from Zeke and go to look out the French doors. I can see my grandparents. Josiah is holding Lila, who I'm pretty sure is crying. Her shoulders are shaking. My heart goes out to her. She couldn't save her sister. It makes me remember Mary and my own fear of not being able to get to her. What if I can't save my sister either?

"Thinking about what?" Zeke pulls my attention back to our conversation.

"My name. Who I am. Who I should be." Taking a deep breath, I plunge into a conversation that's rumbled around in my head for weeks. "I've been Mattie Hathaway, Claire Hathaway's daughter, all my life. The foster kid whose mom tried to kill her. Being Mattie has gotten me nothing but pain and misery."

I turn around so I can face my dad. I've been thinking about this for a while, and I still don't know if this is the right thing to do.

Zeke pours himself some coffee and waits me out. He's starting to get to know me. You can't force me to say anything.

You have to let me do it in my own time. Or Dan told him about my authority issues. Either way, I'm glad he's not pushing me. It gives me time to put my thoughts together.

"Don't get me wrong. My experiences made me the person I am. Growing up in foster care taught me a lot, gave me skills the average person wouldn't have. Those experiences have kept me alive. I don't regret any of it. I'm alive *because* of it. Doesn't mean I want to be the freak foster kid all my life, though."

"You're not a freak, sweetheart. You're a Crane."

I laugh. I can't help it. He sounds so proud of being a Crane, supernatural abilities and all. "I guess that's my point, Zeke. I don't want to feel like a freak anymore. I want to be somewhere I'm accepted and people don't know about my past."

"What are you saying?" Zeke frowns, but he can't hide the spark of hope in his eyes.

"Mary and I talked a lot about New Orleans. North Carolina holds memories for both of us, horrible memories that we can't escape. There's too much here to remind us of those awful days trapped, being tortured. Even my shrink thinks leaving is a good idea."

"You want to come to New Orleans with me?"

"Only if Mary can come. I can't leave her here. Her nightmares are just as bad as mine. I can't abandon her. If you want me to come stay with you, then Mary has to come."

Zeke regards me quietly for a moment. "Mary Cross is welcome in my home for as long as she wants to stay. She and her mother gave you a home, a family when I could not. You love her as much as if you shared the same blood. She's your sister, and therefore she shall be treated as my daughter. If she wishes to come to New Orleans, she's welcome."

"Thank you, Zeke." I turn away so he can't see the tears in my eyes. I don't like to cry. I pride myself on being tear-proof. At least I used to. Meeting Dan changed all that. He softened me up, and then Mary pretty much annihilated any semblance I had of the hardcore girl I used to be. I miss that girl. Nothing bothered her. It was all about me. Now it's more about protecting the people who matter to me.

"We'll get her back. I have people investigating now. If she's above ground, we'll find her."

But she's not. I can feel it. She's in Deleriel's home, and I can't go there. Silas might be able to get me there, though. Should I tell Zeke about his visit last night? Should I tell my father everything? Even the things Silas told me not to? If I am going to trust him, I should tell him things. But there's a reason Silas almost killed Dan so I could lie to my father.

Gah! I don't know what to do anymore. It feels like I'm being pulled in every direction.

"What's wrong, sweetheart?" Zeke lays a hand on my shoulder. "There's something more than Mary and the Malone boy bothering you. I may not have known you long, but you are my child, and I know when you're hurting."

"There are some things about me you don't know. Things that I was warned not to tell you. Things that might make you change your mind about sacrificing me."

He turns me around and tips my head up with his finger. "There is nothing you can tell me that would ever make me harm you. I swear it on my mother's life, Emma Rose. You are my daughter and I will not let any harm come to you."

He sounds so sincere...do I tell him?

"I..."

Zeke's phone goes off. "One moment, *ma petite*." He pulls his phone out and looks at it. Hopefully, it's about Mary or Benny. The frown tugging at his brows makes my gut twist. What if it's something bad?

"Hello...yes, this Ezekiel Crane." He listens for a few minutes and his face gets even whiter. "Of course. I need a few minutes...let me call you back."

He disconnects the call and takes a deep breath. The look of trepidation on his face sets off every internal alarm I have. What happened?"

"Your mother's awake."

Chapter Five

My new phone's weird ring interrupts my panic. Slipping out of Zeke's office, I answer the phone. "Hello?"

"What's wrong?"

Dan's worried voice soothes my rattled nerves like nothing else. "Is there any news about Mary or Benny?"

"No." He's abrupt. "What's wrong with you?"

"Nothing."

"Mattie, I don't have time for this. I've got my hands full. For once, just tell me, and don't make me drag it out of you."

He sounds irritated and tired. Do I really make him pull things out of me?

Maybe I do. "Zeke got a phone call this morning. Georgina's awake."

"Georgina…" He trails off then clears his throat. "Your mom?"

"For all intents and purposes, I guess she is my mother."

"This isn't good."

"Nope." I take a breath. "Zeke's on the phone right now with the nursing home he had her in. She woke up last night, right after Deleriel visited us."

"Why did they wait so long to call?" He pauses and says something to someone. I can't make it out. He sounds like he's outside. There are cars in the background.

"Zeke said she asked them not to call until this morning."

"And they agreed? Isn't Zeke paying the bills? Surely, they'd call…wait, there's more, isn't there?"

Yup, there's always more. "Someone came and picked her up. The home isn't exactly sure what happened. The security cameras seem to have failed. The only thing anyone can say is it was a man who showed up, and they walked out together.

No one even remembers speaking to either of them."

"Someone just waltzed in there and took her out?"

"Pretty much. Zeke thinks maybe some of her family. The Dupres are bad people, worse than the Cranes."

"*Worse than your father?*"

"Yeah, *Officer Dan*, there are worse people out there than my dad."

He's silent, realizing he's pissed me off. I'm sick of everybody putting Zeke down. So what if he's a criminal? He's good to me, and that's all that should matter.

"Sorry, Squirt."

"No worries, just don't be so quick to judge, okay?"

"I promise to try, but I'm a cop, Mattie. It's in my nature to be wary of men like your father."

"I know." And I did. I wouldn't want to change that about him. It keeps him honest. "How did you know something was wrong?"

"I felt it." He yawns. I guarantee he hasn't been to sleep yet, but neither have

I. "Eli is about to jump out of his skin too. I called to calm us both down. You're feeling pretty freaked out and scared right now."

Well, considering Georgina Dupres was going to sacrifice me to Deleriel after torturing me to the point he could feed, I think it's perfectly natural for me to be feeling like this.

"Zeke said…he said Eli…"

"He'll get over it. He's out of his mind with fear. He needs someone to blame, but as soon as he calms down, he'll realize this isn't your fault. This case would have brought James here eventually. You couldn't have prevented that."

"But would Agent Malone have come alone, or would he have uprooted the whole family?"

"That's more my fault, Squirt. They came to get to know me. Don't blame yourself for that."

"Tell him I'm sorry, and that I'm doing everything I can to get Benny back."

"He knows that." Dan pauses to listen to what's being said in the background.

"Mattie, I gotta go. They need me. You good?"

"Yeah, I'm fine. Zeke's overly paranoid, so you can bet I'm safe."

"Don't do anything stupid, Squirt. At least not until I get there, okay?"

"Who, me?"

He chuckles. "Yes, you…I really gotta go. See you in a couple hours. Love you, Squirt."

"Love you too, Officer Dan."

He hangs up without saying bye. A bad habit he's developed recently.

"You're such a liar."

My head swivels around to see Kane lounging against the wall. He's a full-fledged Reaper. One I went toe to toe with and won. He'd come to take Dan's soul, and I refused to let Dan go. Dan's decision to stay with me ended up costing us all a lot. It also put me on Kane's boss's watch list. My reaping abilities are apparently growing at an alarming rate, and the powers that be decided to assign him to be my guide. I scare them, I think. What's Kane want now, though?

He grins, shoving off the wall. He still

has on the same jeans and t-shirt he always wears.

"I'm an expert liar." I flip my brown hair over my shoulder. "What are you doing here, Kane?"

"I can't come see my new bestie?"

My eyes narrow. He's up to something, but what, I don't know.

"No."

"You're no fun." He pushes blond hair out of sparkling green eyes.

"I'm not in the mood, Kane. Too much going on right now."

"I know." He turns somber. "It's why I'm really here. I just wanted to try to lighten the mood."

"What do you know? Is it about Mary or Benny? Tell me!"

"We've been out searching for them. We're fairly certain Mary has been taken to Hell. The child, well, that's a little more complicated."

"Complicated how?"

"You were right in that Deleriel is using a vessel here on this plane. The human he's hijacked conceals him from all of us."

Well, fudgepops.

It seems like the hits just keep coming. First, we can't get to Mary, and now we can't find Deleriel because he hijacked a meat suit, as Dean would call it. Then my murderous mother wakes up and jumps bail. What the heck am I supposed to do? I sink down on the stairs, dejected.

Kane takes a seat beside me. "I'm not going to tell you everything's going to be okay, because it's not. This isn't going to end well for someone, kid. Best you can do is hope is to minimalize the casualties."

"You know, sometimes you sound like you're old enough to be a grandfather, other times you sound like a teenager."

He smiles, the twinkle back in his eyes. "Maybe one day I'll explain it to you, but for now, I have souls to reap. If you need me, just think about me, and I'll come running. Cool?"

"Cool."

And he's gone. Like Silas, Kane poofs away. There one minute, gone the next. I wish it was an ability I would gain, but my human body probably prevents it.

Dang it.

Zeke pops his head out the door. "There you are. Your grandparents are back. Ready to continue the translation?"

"Can we do it a little later?" I am not ready to go back into such a dark place yet. "I want to lay down for a bit. My head's starting to hurt…" I break off, realizing I said the wrong thing.

"Your head? Is the pain like before? Do we need to go back to the hospital?" All this comes out in a rush as Zeke beelines straight for me, his hands cupping my head, twisting it one way and then another as if he can see whatever's wrong.

His blue eyes burn with fear. I open my mouth to assure him I'm fine, it's just because I haven't slept, when something strange happens. Images start to float upward out of nowhere. Images of a little boy standing beside a coffin. Sadness, anger, fear…the emotions emanating from the child are enough to cripple a grown person. His sister. I'm seeing him at his sister's funeral. More flashes swim up to join the tidal pool. Images of him as a teen, as a young man. I see him engage in his criminal empire.

"Emma Rose, are you okay? Speak to me, *ma petite*, please."

The day he met my mother slams into me. She called herself Melissa. Fun, charming, flirty. More and more images of them together, of how content he was. Then I see him in some darkened room; the smell is atrocious. The Oracle. The prophecy. His greed. The knowledge of what he was going to do to me forces me to my knees.

Then my birth skates across my consciousness. The feeling of instant love, protectiveness. Zeke tells me he loves me and that he'll protect me, but I didn't really believe it until now. I can feel it. The warmth of that memory is ripped away, replaced by the anguish of finding me gone, stolen in the middle of the night. I feel like I've been shot and then drowned all at once. It nearly killed him.

I see him. I see beneath the mask of Ezekiel Crane, and I see *him*. Everything he was, is, and shall be. I see it all.

Is this what Silas was talking about last night? The last door in my mind that needed to be opened?

Fudgepops.

Chapter Six

I spend the next hour confessing everything to my father. And I mean everything. You don't see what I just saw and doubt for even a nanosecond he will protect me with his dying breath. There's a lot to tell. I start by telling him about all my run-ins with Silas, and then how he protected me against Zeke's gift of truth serum. I tell him about my fight for Dan's soul, and I tell him what Silas doesn't want me to tell him, about my own gifts, including being able to bring images to life.

And I tell him about what Silas wants from me. How he selectively bred the

Crane and Dupre family to create me. I leave him reeling when I inform him that Georgina may be my flesh and blood mother, but she's not really my mother, that she only housed the being who was. He staggers to a chair when he begins to understand the woman he came to care for was not the monster I described who was prepared to torture me and then feed me to Deleriel, but a woman who loved us both.

"That's why she changed." His voice shakes, and he takes several deep breaths. "Because it really wasn't her?"

"It wasn't. Silas said he's tried to find her over the last few months, but she went into hibernation. Her grief over losing us drove her to ground."

"Why didn't you tell me any of this before?" Confused and a little hurt sum up my dad right about now. I can't look him in the eyes.

"I didn't know you, Zeke. You'd outright admitted you almost killed me to gain power. Everyone kept telling me what a bad person you were. Even Silas warned me not to let you know what I could do. I think he was afraid you'd kill me as well. It wasn't until I saw inside you that I understood how much you loved me and what you would do to protect me."

"I never denied who I was, *ma petite*, but I thought you understood I wouldn't harm you."

"I do now." I give him a lopsided grin. No one will ever make me doubt my dad's intentions toward me again.

He returns my smile, some of the hurt gone. "So, *ma petite*, let's discuss this new ability of yours. It sounds like maybe you're syphoning some of Dan's new ability."

"No. I'm not. That was the first thing I'd thought of too, but this is different. Dan sees things, but not feelings. Well, it's not even feelings, really. It's more like I'm seeing inside your soul, seeing every individual molecule that makes you who you are. Your memories are just a part of that."

"This is confusing." Zeke gets up and pours himself a strong shot of whatever he has in the container on his desk.

Adults seem to always need liquid courage. I hope I never fall into that trap. I'd rather be as clearheaded as I can be. Especially dealing with angels and demons.

"I'm still not sure if it's what Silas kept harping on. He said there was a third part of my heritage I needed to access to be able to deal with Deleriel. He kept trying to get me to see beneath the mask of his last victim."

"They're not victims, *ma petite*." Zeke rebuffs me. "They made a deal with a demon. They knew what they were getting into."

"But did they?" I question. It's something I've thought a lot about. "Did they really understand what they were giving up? Or the price they'd pay when payment came due?"

Zeke purses his lips. "Mattie, some of those people deserve what they get. The things they make deals for..." He breaks off, shaking his head.

"Some of them, yeah. They do. But what about the people who are just desperate to get out of a bad situation?

What about them?"

"There will always be those people, sweetheart. Do they deserve what they get? Probably not, but there's nothing either of us can do about it."

He's right, but it still stinks.

"Do you have any idea what kind of creature my mother might be? Silas was forbidden to tell me. He says I have to figure it out on my own, and I'm betting this new 'looking through the soul' thing is part of that."

"I honestly do not know, *ma petite*, but I will start researching it, and we should have answers in a few days...what?"

I'm shaking my head. I forgot to mention one thing. "Deleriel gave me until tonight, and then he's coming for me."

"A day?" Zeke's hand shakes as he puts down his glass. "We need more time."

"Fallen Angel, remember. We're on his timeline."

"I..." He clears his throat. "We'll figure this out. I promise." There's fear and panic on his face, but I can guarantee mine is worse.

"I know, but right now, I need to sleep. My head is killing me. I've been up for more than twenty-four hours. I just need a cat nap."

"Of course, *ma petite*. Sleep as long as you need to." He comes over and hugs me, kissing me on the head. "We will fix this."

He'll try, but in the end, I don't think there's anything he can do. This is something only I can do. "Thanks, Zeke."

Going upstairs, I check my phone for messages, but nothing. Dan knows how anxious I am. He needs to let me know what's going on with the investigation. Or maybe he forgot I now have a new phone and is texting to the old number. I need to be there with him, in the thick of it. It'd take my mind off my impending doom.

Anything you want.

I let out a bitter laugh. Even if I manage to survive Deleriel, I promised Silas anything he wanted if he could find Mary and Benny. It sounded like a good idea at the time, but now, in the cold light of day, it was an awful decision.

Kicking off my shoes, I crawl into bed and turn over, staring out the window. The blue sky is calm, soothing, almost. If only I wasn't full of dread. Psychotic mother, Fallen Angel, and a demon all after me.

Life pretty much sucks for me.

I start to drift off, my mind full of worries and what-ifs, but that's when I hear it. Shuffling.

Zeke's ghost-proofing is down. Something's in here with me.

I keep my eyes shut. Hopefully, whatever it is will think I'm asleep and go away.

The shuffling gets closer.

The room temperature starts to dip. Icy cold slaps me, and I shudder when it seeps into my bones. It hurts.

The mattress gives, and I stiffen. It's sitting on the bed with me.

Just don't look. It'll go away.

The cold gets worse as it crawls along the bed toward me, ice crystals forming along the bare skin of my arms. My fingers burn, and my teeth chatter. *Please go away.*

It's not going away, though.

It wheezes by my ear.

The rancid smell tickles my nose.

"Mattie."

It knows my name?

Fingernails dig into my arms, and I roll away from it.

The thing staring at me is not a ghost.

It's the black goo thing that followed me to New Orleans.

Fudgepops.

Chapter Seven

~*Dan*~

Noise. It's all I hear. Everyone around me is just a bunch of noise—talking, arguing, crying. I can't process all the emotions. Not right now. I have to do exactly what they taught us to do in the academy. Don't get personal. Stay calm and be objective. Detach yourself.

It was always the easiest part for me. Detach yourself.

How do you detach yourself when it's your family that's in danger, though? I may not have known Benny or the rest of the Malones long, but they *are* my family.

Even Eli, who's blaming the one person he shouldn't. I want to punch him, but I've kept myself under control. Not sure how much longer I can control the urge, though. I think James realized how angry I was becoming, because he sent Eli to check on his mother.

People rush by me, hurrying to complete tasks, but I'm frozen to this spot, unable to move. If I move, this becomes real, and he'll be in the hands of a monster doing awful things to him. Don't get me wrong, I'm worried about Mary too, but Benny's situation is worse. At least to me. He's with a sadistic pedophile. My mind shies away, refusing to focus on something that will torture it.

"You okay?"

Caleb's question forces me out of my self-imposed silence. He looks haggard, his eyes bloodshot. Like me, he's still wearing the same clothes from last night. Panic and fear seem to have taken up permanent residence in his eyes. Benny is his main priority, but he's worried about Mary too. He likes her a lot. We'd had a conversation about his feelings just a few days ago.

"I'm good. How are you holding up?" Lies, but they are necessary lies. Caleb needs someone who's not about to fall apart. I can do that for him, just like I do for Squirt. James is so busy trying to tear the city apart, he's forgotten his oldest still needs him.

"I could be better. Eli said you checked on Mattie?"

I don't know how Caleb feels about Mattie and her role in all this. I'm not up to arguing, but I can't refuse to answer. "She's okay, considering."

"What was wrong? You two were about to come out of your skin."

"Her mother woke up."

"That's a good thing, isn't it?"

My eyes scan the neighborhood, searching each car that passes. I know he's not in any of them, but it distracts my mind. "No. Her mother promised Mattie's soul to Deleriel. She's been trapped in a prison of her own mind by Deleriel for over fifteen years."

"So…not good, then." Caleb lets out a

long, deep sigh. "Think we'll ever catch a break?"

Probably not.

"Look, I'm going to head over to Zeke's and see if Mattie's up to doing that sketch."

"Didn't you do one already?" Caleb frowns, his eyes scrunching up in confusion. "They were passing them out earlier."

"Yeah, but that was me trying to describe something I could barely make out. I'm hoping Mattie can see what I see. I'd trust her drawings over anyone else's."

"How can she see what you see?"

"I don't know if she can, but I'm going to try. At least it's something I can do. Plus, I need to check on her. Make sure she's not doing anything stupid."

Whatever you want.

Her vow to Silas. I'm not about to let her give her soul away. Not for anyone or anything. Knowing her, she probably believes she deserves whatever happens to her. She takes on the blame for everything.

"Mind if I come along?" Caleb shifts from foot to foot, nervous energy radiating off him. "I need to be doing something. All this standing around and watching everyone run circles around each other is getting to me."

"I don't know…"

"Look, I'm not Eli. I don't blame her for anything. It's not Mattie's fault."

"Okay. You're driving, then. I was going to call Dad to come pick me up."

"When are they going to let you drive again?"

"I have a follow-up with the neuro guy in two weeks." We start walking down the street to where Caleb's parked. We pass the mobile command unit where my captain is giving orders. She briefly glances my way and nods. I jerk my head in response. She'd ordered me to stand down since my family was involved. It's why I feel so useless. No one will tell me anything.

"Slow down a sec." Caleb grabs my arm, pulling me to a stop. I look at him in askance. He's sweeping the street, deserted, for the most part. It's early.

Most everyone is at work. A jogger passes us on the other side of the street.

"What?" There's nothing unusual here.

"Don't you feel it?" Caleb whispers. "There's something here, watching us."

"No."

"You're still new to this, and you aren't trained. Trust me when I tell you there's something here, something that wants to hurt us."

Caleb's the expert, so I'm going to trust him. "Can we make it to your truck?"

"I think so." He starts walking again, much slower, and he never stops searching the shadows. "Don't look with your eyes. Look with your senses."

"What does that even mean?" I'm about as much Luke Skywalker as he is Yoda.

"It means stop thinking what you see is all there is. Look for what's *not* there."

That makes a little more sense, especially to my police officer's brain. We're trained to look for what's not there.

The first thing I notice is the absence

of sound. There doesn't even seem to be any traffic on this particular block. There are no pets outside, no one sitting on front porches or talking on the sidewalks. The place is still as death. It's mid-morning, but there should still be people milling about.

Caleb's right. Something is definitely not right.

Closing my eyes, I listen. The silence is eerie, the complete lack of sound disturbing. A feeling creeps over me, something hard to define. I've gotten it a few times on the job. It's almost like a finger trailing down your spine, telling you that you're about to walk into something dangerous. It's not something we learn at the academy. Instead, it's what we learn on the job. We trust our instincts, and in this instance, something is out here, watching us. I feel it. Eyes roving over me, around me, daring me to move.

And there's something else. Something dark and cold...but the cold is a scam. Mattie says cold means a ghost, but this thing, whatever it is, wants us to think it's a ghost, but every instinct I have says it's not.

Sulphur. I smell sulphur. My eyes snap open, and I take in everything around me. The silent street, the still window curtains in the homes around us. The sun has fled, giving way to the cloudy sky. It's caused the street to be bathed in semi-darkness.

"It's a demon."

"How do you know?" Caleb cracks his knuckles, preparing for a fight.

"Can't you smell the sulphur?" Come on, where are you? I look for a spot that is darker than the rest, but with the street shaded, it's hard to find one instance where it's darker than anywhere else.

"Uh...no." He sounds unsure, but I know what I smell. It's a scent I will never forget, thanks to Silas. That demon is going to eventually die by my hands, but not until we get Mattie out of her current death sentence. I need him to help her.

"There." I take a step toward an old Honda parked on the side of the street. The shadows are deeper around it than any other vehicle. "Whatever it is, it's behind that car."

"I don't see anything."

I chuckle, despite the seriousness of the situation. Caleb may be a hunter, but he's not a cop. I might have only been on the force for less than a year, but I have been trained to think like one.

"The shadows are darker there than anywhere else on the street."

Caleb squints and studies the spot. "You're right."

"See, even the cop can teach the seasoned hunter a thing or two. Now, the real question is are we prepared to deal with whatever kind of demon it is, or do we make a run for your truck?"

"You can't run from them."

"Okay, so how do we deal with it then?"

Caleb doesn't answer right away. The frown on his face is telling, though. He's worried.

"It's tricky. I don't know what kind of demon it is."

"That's important?"

"Yeah, very. What works for one doesn't necessarily work for another. I usually have my sword that's been blessed, but I don't take it with me everywhere. Blessed swords can usually at least scatter them, if not kill them."

"Your truck is just around the corner. You sure we can't make a run for it?" I have no desire to face a demon unarmed, especially if Caleb looks this grim.

"It can hear us."

I wondered why he wasn't whispering. No point if the thing's hearing is that good. "It would be waiting for us."

"Yes."

"What do we do?"

"Pray."

Caleb squares his shoulders and strides toward the Honda. What is he doing? I hurry to catch up. "You got a plan?"

"No."

He keeps walking and I'm scrambling to come up with a plan. You don't go into a hostile situation without a plan or backup. That's how you get killed.

"We can't just..." My words trail off when a dark shadow detaches itself from the car. Inky blackness is all we see at first. It's hunched in on itself. The spasmodic jerking sets off alarm bells. Slowly, it raises its head, the white face almost like a mask if it wasn't staring at me with such evil in its expression. Another jerk, and it's closer.

I know this thing.

I've seen it before.

The demon who attacked us right before Mattie ran to New Orleans.

Chapter Eight

"We need a weapon."

Iron, maybe? I really need to get some kind of weapon made out of iron that's easy to carry around. Now that I'm aware of the things that go bump in the night, they're aware of me too.

"It's the same demon that followed Mattie to New Orleans."

"I remember. It's a protection demon. We never did figure out who sent the first one after her."

"It's here with us, though, so is it protecting you from me or me from you?"

"Or maybe it's the same one from New

Orleans? We never killed it."

"That doesn't make sense." I shake my head, eyeballing the thing. More black goo drips from its clenched hands, making a wet plot on the pavement. "We haven't seen it since New Orleans, and that was weeks ago."

"I know, I'm just trying to sort it out."

"Why isn't it moving?" It's stopped, staring at us. Black liquid seeps from its eyes, and I cringe away from it.

"I don't know." Caleb inches closer to me.

"*Mattie....*"

"Why is it saying Mattie's name?"

Caleb's question is lost as this overwhelming sense of dread creeps along my spine. A rancid odor invades my nose, and I shudder. Dizzy. The world starts spinning, and I'm no longer standing on the street facing a very dangerous demon. I'm in my room at Zeke's. Only it's not me. I'm seeing Mattie sitting up in the bed, the demon on the bed beside her.

Reaching out to her.

She tries to scramble away, but it

snakes out a hand and grabs her hand, freezing her in place. Laughter. The thing is laughing.

Someone shakes me, but I can't move. It has its hands on her. On me.

She tries to draw a breath, but she can't. She's frozen, unable to even make her lungs work. Black goo seeps up her arms, over her shoulders, and around her neck, strangling her. It's killing her.

"Dan!"

Caleb shoves me backward, breaking whatever connection I had with Mattie. He's hauling me back as fast as he can, but if we get away, she's dead. My head swivels to stare at the creature smiling at us.

Mattie's soul is bound with mine. Maybe this thing is connected to the demon with Mattie. It hasn't tried to hurt us. Maybe it's a shade of the demon in her room? Without thinking, I push Caleb away and reach for my sword.

The demon hisses when it sees the sword, and I smile. Power surges through me and I stride toward it, more confident than I've ever been in my life. This is going to work. It's a truth I feel in every bone in my body.

Its expression morphs into one of fear, and it's going to disappear. I know this like I know the sun will rise every morning. Not this time. My feet move with a speed that is foreign to me, but it takes me less than a second to reach the demon. Swinging, I watch the sword slice through the inky blackness. A wail fills the air around us as I pull my sword back and sink the blade deep into the center of its chest.

Claws dig into my flesh, but I press forward, twisting the blade and pushing it as far as I can. The demon explodes into a mess of black liquid, its scream echoing around us in the emptiness of the street.

Without waiting, I dig out my phone and call Squirt. *Please, please pick up.* Her voicemail.

No, wait. She has a new number.

Looking through my recent calls, I find her and hit dial, holding my breath.

"Dan?"

Her voice is soft, ragged.

"Is it still there?"

"No." She clears her throat. "It exploded. I…Dan…I couldn't breathe, couldn't move, couldn't call out."

"I know. I saw you."

"You saw me?"

"This new vision thing I have, maybe? I don't know how I saw you, I just did. The demon-thing was here too."

"Are you okay?" True fear coats her words.

"I'm good, Squirt. This sword comes in handy. Caleb and I are on our way over. Go find your dad and stay with him until we get there."

"Okay, but hurry."

"We will. See you soon." I hang up and turn to find my brother staring at me in something akin to fear and awe. It makes me a little uncomfortable. "You ready to go?"

He nods and starts walking toward the truck, pulling out his own phone to text while he walks. Probably either Eli or his father.

My phone starts buzzing, and I answer it without looking, thinking it's Mattie.

"What's wrong with her?"

Eli's frantic voice all but yells into my ear.

"Demon. She's fine now, though." Not like he cares. He's blaming her for everything. It's the Guardian Angel bond. He can't ignore it, no matter how much he wishes otherwise.

"She's not fine. I can feel her fear." There's an edge in his voice, which only confirms my suspicions about his hating the bond they share.

"Of course, she's afraid. She just got attacked by a demon. She's with her dad, though. Zeke will protect her. If you don't believe me, call her."

Not sure why I'm suggesting it, but I know she'd feel better if he called. She's tearing herself to pieces thinking he hates her. I'll swallow my own pride if it means taking away some of her pain.

"No, as long as you're sure she's okay."

"I'm sure."

"Call me if anything comes up."

He hangs up before I can say anything else. He needs to get over this blame game. None of us has time for it.

"I let Dad know what happened. He says to keep your sword close. It's the only thing that can kill a protection demon. Nothing we have will kill one. The iron shotgun shells only wound it."

We climb into the truck and I lay the sword across my lap so I can buckle up. It pulses against my hand. The thing almost seems alive. It's creepy, really, but it doesn't *feel* creepy. It feels right, like an extension of me.

"It suits you."

"What does?"

"The sword." Caleb puts the truck into gear and pulls out. "It magnifies everything good within its wielder. It makes your strengths greater and gives you the edge you need in battle. You look like a warrior holding it."

I wouldn't go that far, but it does feel right in my hands.

Time for a subject change. "Is there a way to find out who sent that demon? Mattie has problems protecting herself against it."

"Mattie?"

I explain to him my theory of the

demon who was here being a shade of the one with Mattie. Worry blinks like flashing neon lights in Caleb's expression. "They're not supposed to do that."

"There a crap ton of stuff that isn't supposed to work like they do. The thing almost killed her. Her demon exploded the same time ours did. Her soul is connected to mine, and now with this new vision thing, I think that's what happened."

Caleb frowns. "It makes sense, but they usually only show up when the person they're protecting is around the target."

"Weird."

"Very," Caleb agrees. "Who would want you protected from Mattie, though?"

A sinking suspicion starts to grow. She wouldn't.

But it did stop in New Orleans right after…

"Caleb, we need to make a pit stop."

"Where?"

"My parents'."

Chapter Nine

I start to open the truck door, but pause. Caleb is staring at my house, his face a mask of trepidation. I want to kick myself. I should have waited until later to do this. How is it so easy for me to forget that my mother killed his?

"I can do this later. Why don't we head over to Mattie's?"

Caleb shakes his head, his eyes never leaving the house. "No. I'm going to have to face her eventually. You need to talk to her about the protection demon. If you're right, and we don't stop her, she'll only send another one after your girl."

I should correct him about Mattie

being my girl, but the truth is, I like the way it sounds.

"I don't want to believe Mom would do something like this. She's adamant about taking me to protect me from all that. Why would she be calling on the same creatures she despises?"

"People do all sorts of strange things to protect the people they love, Dan. Your mother sees Mattie as a major threat to your safety. The Sterlings have always been a powerful family in the supernatural world. She'd know how to do this."

"Are you sure you're up for this? You don't have to come in."

"No. I want to. Mattie needs as many people in her corner as she can get. My first instincts are to protect her, and that's what I'm going to do."

The Malone family were bred to protect living reapers. It really is Caleb's first instinct to protect her because it's in his blood to do so. When we first met, Caleb bodily prevented me from getting near Squirt because of the hurt I'd caused her.

"If it gets to be too much, we can leave. She's my mom, but you're my brother too. I don't want you hurt because of her any more than you already are."

"I'm good. Are you sure *you* want to do this, though? Your dad just parked on the sidewalk."

My head swivels, and sure enough, my father is getting out of his car, frowning at the strange truck in his driveway. Why did he have to come home now? Dad is firmly grounded in reality and already thinks my mom's a nutcase because of her talk of how evil the Malones are.

"Freaking great."

Caleb laughs. "You sound like Mattie."

I smile. I guess she's rubbing off on me more than I'd thought. I climb out of the truck, and Dad's frown eases.

"Dan. What are you doing here? Is Mattie okay?"

Unlike Mom, Dad adores Squirt. He wanted her to come live here after her ordeal with Mrs. Olson, her serial killer foster mother, but Mom refused, stating she didn't want a violent child in the house. In reality, she knew exactly who Mattie was, and instead of honoring her promise to her sister to keep her child safe, she let her rot in foster care. That's how much she despises Mattie.

"No, Dad, she's not." No point in trying to ease him into this. He's not going to take it well anyway.

"What happened?"

"She was attacked."

"Attacked?" His face pales. "Did an orderly...or..."

"She's not in the hospital, Dad. They released her this morning. She's home with Zeke."

"Then how was she attacked?"

"That's what we're here to find out, Mr. Richards." Caleb has gotten out of the truck and come to stand beside me.

"Caleb...I don't understand. Why would you come here to find that out?"

"We think Mom had something to do with it." There, I said it. Dad's face goes from confusion to even more bewildered.

"Ann hurt Mattie?" He shakes his head. "No. She wouldn't do that, Dan. She knows how much Mattie means to you."

"If she thought Mattie posed a threat to Dan, she might, sir." Caleb looks like he wants to be anywhere but here having this conversation. Not that I blame him. I don't want to have it either.

"No."

"Dad, Caleb's right. She's hurt people before to protect me, and she hates Mattie. We just need to talk to her, and if she had nothing to do with this, then she didn't. But I need to know one way or another."

The pain that flickers through my father's expression guts me. I hate doing this to him, driving one more nail into coffin of the woman who's shared his life for over two decades. It's heartbreaking, but I can't let myself think about that. I have to know if my mom is responsible for the protection demon.

Plastering on my cop face, as Mattie calls it, I wait. When Dad nods, I turn and walk into the house, he and Caleb right behind me.

"Mom?" I call out, kicking my shoes off. It's habit. She's never let us wear our shoes in the house. I've been on carpet cleaning duty more than once because I forgot. She once made Cam clean every floor downstairs during his first year of marriage because he tracked mud into the front hall. She has this look of disappointment that brings us all to our knees. One more thing I'm going to have to guard against over the next few minutes.

"Dan?"

I look toward the stairs and see her coming down, a smile on her face. It falters when she sees who's behind me. She has to know who Caleb is. He looks just like me.

"Mom, come into the kitchen. We need to talk." I don't give her time to react to Caleb, just head for the kitchen. I nod to Caleb to take a seat at the island and open the fridge. I grab a bottle of water, asking Caleb if he wants one. He shakes his head, clearly uncomfortable.

"Ann. No, I don't know why he's here…" I hear Dad and Mom speaking quietly as they follow us. "Dan has some questions for you."

Instead of sitting at the island, Mom takes a seat at the kitchen table. Her eyes dart between Caleb and me, her expression pained. She doesn't want him here any more than he wants to be here. Tough. She's going to have to get used to him. He's my brother, and he's going to be a part of my life. Even if they're never able to get past what she did, she's still going to have to deal with the Malones being my family as much as she is.

"Mom, this is my brother, Caleb Malone."

She doesn't say anything, but her expression hardens.

"Mrs. Richards." Caleb nods his head politely. One hand is fisted so tight, his knuckles are white. Maybe Caleb should have stayed in the truck.

"Why is he here?" Her blunt question fuels my anger, but I do my best to hold it in check.

"He's here to support me."

Her eyes narrow. "Support you?"

"I have to ask you some questions, Mom."

"If this is about…" She stops and takes

a breath. "I'm not answering any questions about...about...New Orleans."

"You mean about how you murdered my mother?" The anger and the hurt bleeding out of him is as heartbreaking as the pain on my father's face.

"I did what I had to do to protect an innocent child."

"And what about the child you left motherless?" Caleb's other fist clenches. "What about the pain you caused me?"

"It was too late for you. You were tainted."

Not even an "I'm sorry" to help sooth Caleb's pain.

"Ann!" Dad's gasp of outrage makes her look over at him.

"What?" she asks. "I'm only speaking the truth. They're evil, Earl. You may never believe me, but they are."

"We are *not* evil." Caleb's voice has gone quiet. "My family has never dealt in demons or dark magic. Can you say the same?"

That announcement causes Dad to gape at Caleb. This is what I was afraid of. Dad's going to think we're all crazy.

108

"Everyone calm down and take a step back." My training kicks in, and I become the mediator. I can't let this situation spiral out of control. "Caleb, if this is too hard, then go outside and wait in the truck. I can do this myself."

"I'm good." Caleb forces himself to visibly relax, but one hand remains clenched tight. I can't imagine the pain he's in right now, but he's here for me.

"Dad, there are a few things you need to understand. Doesn't matter if you believe it or not, but for this discussion, you'll have to accept it as truth."

"Dan?" Dad's hesitant questioning almost makes me ask him to go outside too. I don't want to shatter his illusions. It's unpleasant to have your entire belief in the world pulled out from under you. It can't be helped, though. He's my father, and he needs to know the truth. It might even help his relationship with Mom to know she's not crazy.

"Mom's not crazy. The things that go bump in the night? The supernatural world? It's all real. Ghosts, demons, angels. All of it is as real as you and me."

He frowns, his confusion deepening. "Dan, that's just not true."

"But it is, Dad. James works for the spook squad of the FBI. They go out and deal with all that stuff. Caleb's a trained hunter. He's been dealing with this since he was a kid."

"No..." Dad shakes his head again, refusing to believe.

"I can't deny what I've seen with my own two eyes."

"You've seen them?" He lets out a ragged breath, and I start to worry. His heart's not that good. Mom's been worried about him.

"Yes."

"Tell me." He leans back, running a shaky hand through his hair. I hand him my unopened bottle of water, which he accepts.

"Earl, are you okay?" Mom grips his hand, as worried as I am. His breathing has sped up a bit. Maybe this was too much stress to drop on him.

"Dad?" I squat down in front of him, concern morphing into panic when he wheezes a bit. "Maybe we should take him to the E.R."

"No." Dad waves us off. "I'm fine."

"You don't look fine, Mr. Richards." Caleb reaffirms my own suspicions Dad needs a doctor. "Maybe you should go to the hospital."

"I said I was fine."

"Earl…"

"Dan, go on with your story. I don't know if I believe this or not, but I want to hear why you think your mother is involved in this."

I want to argue with him, but I know him. He's as stubborn as I am, and he's not going to budge until I tell him what he wants to know. So, I spend the next hour telling him about all of it. Mattie being a reaper and part demon, her family and their heritage as well as the Malones'. I tell him about my own personal experiences, especially about Silas and the reaper Mattie fought to keep me here when I was supposed to die. He looks ready to throw up when I explain I had a choice to go or stay, and I chose to stay because of Squirt.

"I…I don't know what to say."

"It's a lot, I know. It took me months to come to terms with it all." I go get another bottle of water for myself. Mom and Caleb both shake their heads when I offer them one. "Mom's not crazy, Dad. I promise."

"She's really not." Caleb stands up. "She may be a lot, but she's not crazy."

Mom's eyes narrow, but I stop her before she can say anything. "Which brings us to why we're here."

"You think Ann had something to do with the attack on Mattie."

He's staring at my mom, silently begging her to have no part in this, but I have a sinking suspicion she does. She looks too defiant.

"She was attacked by a protection demon in New Orleans. I almost forgot about it until the thing showed up again earlier. It almost killed her."

"Protection demon?" Dad's eyes squint as he tries to sort it. It's the same expression I had when I heard it for the first time.

"Yes. Someone called a demon up to kill her in order to protect someone else."

"And you think your mother did that to protect you?"

I wish I could protect him from this, but I can't. If Mom's responsible…heck, I don't know. What am I supposed to do if she is?

"Are you, Mom? Did you call up a demon to protect me from her?"

She sits there, refusing to answer, and I know I'm right. It's in her eyes. She looks gleeful. She knows it won't stop until it's killed Mattie.

"It makes sense." Caleb cracks his knuckles. "It stopped when you went to jail and only started up again now, when you think she's involving Dan in the world you fought to keep him out of."

"That girl is evil." Mom fidgets, her eyes glinting with a hint of madness. "I've asked you again and again to leave her alone, but you won't listen. You're determined to get yourself killed to protect something that is truly vile. She's part demon. You said so yourself. She's unclean."

"She's no more evil than I am." Dad slams his hand against the table, startling us all. "She is just a child who's never known anything but pain, and yet she survived it. She loves our son. You heard him tell you how she fought to keep him here. He's alive because of her, Ann. She gave us our child, and you call her evil?"

"She's unclean."

"Is that why you let her rot in foster care?" I ask softly. "She was your sister's daughter, the child you swore to protect, but abandoned. Why do you hate her so much, Mom?"

"She's the reason my sister is dead. Of course, I hate her. I begged Amanda to leave her alone, begged her to think about it, but she refused to see reason. My sister died protecting that thing."

"She's not a thing." My spine straightens even more than it was. "I love her. She's my family as much as you or Caleb are."

"She is not your family!" My mom jumps up and starts to pace. "She's a demon. Don't you understand what that means?"

"Yeah, Mom, I do, but that doesn't change who she is. She's still the same

person she was when I met her a year
ago. She's kind and loyal, tough as nails,
and will go to bat for the people she
loves. She's the only person who stood
up for you when we found out you
murdered Amelia. She told me to call
you, to warn you. No one else had your
back, not even me. The cop in me
wouldn't let me have your back, but she
did. That's how evil she is."

"It was a ploy."

"Do you know what you sound like?"
Disgusted, Dad gets up and walks over to
lean against the island. "She's done
nothing but protect our son."

"Did you send the protection demon
after her?" Caleb brings the conversation
back around to the original question.

"I won't let her hurt Dan."

"But by sending that thing after her,
you are hurting Dan." Caleb clenches and
unclenches his fists. "Not just
emotionally, but physically."

"What are you talking about?"

"Mattie's soul is tied to mine, Mom. If
she dies, then so do I."

Her face pales. "No. It's not possible."

"My soul got tethered to hers when she hid me from the reaper. Then the Angel tied us together for eternity. I'm not supposed to be here, Mom. Mattie's the only thing keeping me on this world. If you kill her, then you kill me. What don't you understand about that?"

Her head drops into her hands, and her shoulders start to shake. She's crying. My first instinct is to comfort her, but I resist. I keep my cop face on. This has to be settled now. She can't keep doing this.

"Did you do it? Did you send the protection demon after her, Mom?"

"Yes."

Her whispered confession sets my blood to boiling, and I want to shout, to scream, to tell her I never want to see her again. Suspecting and hearing her admit to it are two entirely different things. I wasn't prepared for the sudden anger that consumes me. She lied. Does she even know how to speak the truth anymore?

One second I'm fuming, and the next I'm standing there with sword in my hand, its blade inches from her neck. It is the Sword of Truth, and it stands in

judgement of liars. It wants to judge her.
I can feel the blade's need to taste her
flesh.

"Dan. Put the sword down."

"Where did that thing come from?"

I take two steps, and the blade is
against her bare skin. Her lies dance up
the blade and sink into my skin. I can see
everything she's done, and she has done
some truly terrible things. It all flashes
like a movie across my field of vision.

"Dan, I know the sword wants you to
judge her, but she's your mother. If you
judge her, it will kill her. Don't let the
sword take control of you." Caleb lays
his hand on my shoulder. It grounds me,
and I can see past the need to let the steel
taste her guilt. I see my mother, her head
bowed, shaking. Stumbling backward, I
let the sword fall out of my hands.

"I…how did that happen?"

"It's the sword." Caleb keeps his voice
calm and even. "It knows when you're
struggling. She lied to you, and then
when you discovered her lies, it hurt. The
sword rose up to defend you, to defend
the truth. It wanted to judge her lies, and

if she was found lacking, it would have killed her."

"I don't want that thing anymore."

I stare at it, lying there against the white tile of the kitchen floor. Fear creeps along my spine. I almost killed my mother.

"It doesn't matter." Caleb leans down and picks it up. "The Angel gave it to you because he knows you can see through the lies and find the truth. The sword bonded with you. It will be yours until the day you can no longer carry its burden."

"Someone needs to explain to me how that thing got here." My dad stares from the sword to me and back again.

"It's called the Sword of Truth. It was given to Dan by an Archangel. It's always there, even when it's not. All he has to do is reach for it. It's a Holy Warrior's sword."

"That day at the cemetery when the priest said he saw the outline of the sword on your back…this is what he meant?"

I nod. "He used to have one of the

Holy Swords. That's how he knew what I needed to do to open the crypt door to save Mattie."

"And when they told me to drag Mattie out, that it would help you…" Dad cuts off, sinking down onto one of the bar stools. "You were better the minute I got her out of the crypt."

"Yes. There was a ghost, one that had been tortured by a Fallen Angel's proxy until its soul was so battered, it died. There was nothing left of it, and it was killing her. You broke the contact between her and the child, saving both Dan and Mattie in the process."

"This can't be real."

"Now do you see, Earl? Do you see what I saved our son from? This madness, vile, evil things these people deal in, and that girl…she's the worst one of them all."

My mom's eyes are bright with her own madness. She's never going to understand that Mattie isn't evil, that she's the best person I know. Nothing will ever change her mind.

"Mom. I'm saying this once and only

once. You will never do a thing to hurt her again. If you do, I will walk away from you." I go to stand in front of her so she has to look me in the eyes. "I will cut you out of my life forever. Do you understand?"

"You would choose her over me?" Tears well up in my mother's eyes, tears that tear me apart, but I am serious. She has to stop this.

"When it comes to Mattie, yeah, Mom, I would. Her life is tied to mine. You hurt her, you hurt me. Doesn't matter how much you hate her, you have to stop this because you're going to kill me. If you love me at all, you will stop sending demons after her. You have to promise me here and now, or we're done."

"Daniel…"

"No." I refuse to back down on this. She's going to get me killed. "You keep harping on how evil the Malones are, but they've never summoned a demon to my knowledge. The only parent I know who's done that is you."

"You don't know that…"

"We don't deal in demons." Caleb

stops her before she can form the sentence. "Our job is to hunt down demons and either kill them or send them back to where they came from. We don't summon them to help us in any way, shape, or form. We're hunters, not black magic wielders. You have it backwards, Mrs. Richards. We aren't evil. We protect people *from* evil."

She looks like she wants to argue, but Caleb's right. The only evil right now is the woman in front of me. Yes, she might be trying to protect me, but she's becoming the very thing she fought so hard to keep me away from. "Mom. I know you love me and you do what you think is best, but summoning a demon to kill Mattie? That's the only evil I see right now."

"He's right, Ann. You are the only person who has done anyone harm. You might have done it for the right reasons, but this is wrong. If you called on something to hurt Mattie, you need to stop it. I'm not sure what I believe, but I know that child is special, and she deserves the happiness you denied her.

You owe your sister that much."

"Please, Mom."

"I'll call it off." Her shoulders sag in defeat.

"The one you sent is dead. The sword took care of it. I just need you to promise not to send any more after her. She has enough to worry about right now."

"I promise."

"Thank you." I kiss her on the cheek.

"All I've ever done was to protect you, Dan. I swear."

"I know."

Stepping back, I take a deep breath. Now that this is taken care of, I need to go check on Squirt and see if she's up to trying to test this connection we have. It might just save Benny if she can.

Chapter Ten

~*Mattie*~

Zeke is on the phone when I come downstairs. It sounds important, so I don't want to disturb him. Instead, I wander into the kitchen, my stomach growling. I'm starved. Even though Mrs. Banks served a full breakfast earlier, I only picked at the food, listening to Josiah translate one of the books about living reapers.

"Hey, there, Miss Mattie." Mrs. Banks beams at me. She's wearing a skirt and sweater today. More for my grandparents than anything. She's a jeans and t-shirt kinda girl, just like me. "You hungry?"

"Starved." I give her a small smile, still shaken by the demon that appeared in my room.

"You okay?"

No, not really. I can still feel that black goo crawling up my arms and snaking around my throat, squeezing. My hand goes up to my throat, trying to ward off the sensations. Mrs. Banks gasps and hurries over, brushing my hand out of the way. "What happened?"

"There was something in my room." I wrap my arms around myself, feeling just as terrified as I was earlier.

"Oh, my poor girl." Mrs. Banks hugs me and leads me over to the table. She pushes my hair out of the way and examines my neck. I'm sure there's a nasty mark. "What was it?"

"A protection demon."

"What?"

The startled gasp pulls my attention to the doorway where Josiah is standing. He looks more than a little alarmed.

"How do you know about protection demons?" He strides in, and Mrs. Banks moves out of the way so he can examine the damage the demon did.

"One attacked me in New Orleans."

"When were you in New Orleans?" Josiah questions as he frowns at the red marks I can only assume are there.

"I went down there with Doc to check out a haunted house. It's where I met the Malones and found out about Zeke."

The image of the demon rises, and I shrink back, unable to stop the full body shudder it causes. I couldn't do anything to stop it. I still don't know what stopped it.

"Easy, Mattie." Josiah's voice is low and soothing. "You're safe now."

"No, I'm not," I whisper. "I'll never be safe."

"Here." Mrs. Banks sets a sandwich down in front of me, along with a can of Coke. "It's a BLT. I had some leftover bacon from breakfast."

"Thank you."

"Did you tell your father?" Josiah takes a seat beside me and asks for a cup of coffee and a sandwich if there's any more bacon left.

I shake my head. "He was busy, so I came in here. I didn't want to be by myself."

"You father is never too busy for you, *ma petite chou*. None of us are."

Words. Just words. I've never been anyone's priority. Being alone up in that room with no one to help me brought that home. The only person who can protect me is me. No one else. My dad cares, but he can't be everywhere. Not even in his fortress. For all his gifts and magical wards, things can still get through.

"You know that, don't you, Mattie?" Josiah's soft question has me nodding, the movement wooden. It's what he needs to hear. I wish I believed him, but twelve years in foster care does things to you. A few days of hearing "I love you" isn't going to erase a decade of the contrary.

"Will you read to me?" Best to get him off this line of questioning. "I want to hear more from the journal. It'll take my mind off everything."

"We need to figure out who sent the demon after you, sweetheart. I can't stop it if I don't know who sent it."

"It's gone. I don't want to think about it anymore. Please."

I hate feeling helpless, and that's what memories of that thing does to me. Anything to push it out of my mind for a little while.

"Okay, *ma petite chou*, but we will need to speak with your papa about this."

I nod and let out a sigh of relief when Josiah gets up and goes in search of the journal. The more I know about my own reaping abilities, the better. They may not help me defeat Deleriel or get Mary and Benny back, but they might help me beat death. One thing the powers that be have planned for me the minute I take care of Deleriel.

Knowledge is power, and I have less than twelve hours to figure all this out.

Chapter Eleven

5 October, 1539

We rode through Donna's hamlet on our way out of the lands surrounding the Sept. I felt the need to bear witness to the horror visited upon the people I only sought to help. It is a memory I must bear all my life, and I can only hope to one day atone for the slaughter.

The barren buildings have already begun to look abandoned and left for the wilderness to reclaim. The small hamlet is silent. No animals scurry. No birds fly overheard or can be heard chirping. This place has been condemned. The animals know it.

Whispers come to us on the wind, screams echoing along the silent roads. It is my own imagination doing this, I know, but it doesn't make it any easier to face the fact I did this.

The church looms ahead of us, its charred remains a glowering testament to the depravity carried out here. Father Galen slows his horse, his face a mask of torment. I cannot even begin to imagine what he must be feeling, the memories this must stir. I should not have come here, not with the Father. This will only cause him unnecessary pain.

A man steps from the burned church. He's wearing a heavy cloak, the hood completely obscuring his face. At his side walks Donna, or what once was the girl. She is a shade of her former self, the burns on her little body abundant. Her eyes are strange. They glow yellow. And they do not recognize me.

Who is this man, and how did the

child survive?

Father Galen begins to murmur, and I recognize the prayer he chants. He's afraid. Whoever this man is, he terrifies the Father.

I push my steed forward, approaching the two of them. The man pauses and turns to look at me. I can feel his eyes on me even if I cannot see his face. It is unnerving. I demand to know who is and what he's doing with the child.

His response is chilling. Feeding. He's feeding from his child.

His child.

Donna shows no outward signs of pain. She simply stares at me, a hunger in her eyes that should not be there. It's a desperate kind of hunger, one that makes me want to turn my horse around and flee, but I cannot. I am rooted to the spot.

He shoves his hood back, and my instincts scream at me to run from the evil staring at me, but I am a trained

Historian. I will not fail the Church.

I demand to know who he is.

His face is beautiful. Angelic. His amber eyes look through me and pierce my soul. I feel it. His hand is on my soul. I shiver, but refuse to back down.

"You are not meant for this world," he tells me. "You shouldn't be here."

Nor should he, I tell him.

He laughs, his hand on the child's head. He leans down and whispers something to her, and she nods, her eyes centered on me in a way a hunter's would be on its prey. More children begin to file out of the church, surrounding him, their little bodies ravaged by fire.

I do back up this time. They all look so...hungry.

"They belong to me now." The man walks down the steps, the children following. When he takes the reins of my horse from me, I try to jump, but his hand clamps down on my thigh. "You will remember me from this life and into the next, Sylvia Fields. When I come to claim you, you will know me."

He and his children vanish, but the imprint of his hand remains upon my skin and my soul. What has he done to me?

3 January, 1540

My mind has been splintered these last weeks. I am unable to focus, to find meaning in anything. Not since the day at the church. Father Galen swore me to silence. He said the Church would not understand what happened. I'm not even sure myself what happened. The need to confess grows hourly, but what if Father Galen is right? Will the Church choose to cleanse me as they did him, or will they just burn the sin from me?

Those amber eyes haunt me, from the waking world into my slumbers. I feel unclean, and I need to confess.

What did he mean, I did not belong in this world? Or his order to remember him from one life to the next? Who or what is he?

I do not think there is anything holy about him. He reeked of evil. Why would I need to remember him? It has confused me greatly. Perhaps Father Galen will hear my confession, since he warned me against speaking to the Bishop about it?

Will confessing to Father Galen be enough? Will it cleanse this burden from my soul, or must it be cleansed through fire? I am not an innocent child. I am a woman grown who knows her own mind. I am not clean. I need forgiveness, as only my confessor assigned to guide me can give absolution.

Chapter Twelve

"Well, what happened?" I lean forward, curious to see what Sylvia would do. I have no doubts as to who she met. It had to be Deleriel. Why hadn't Heather, Eli's mom and the Malone family Historian, caught that?

"I don't know." Josiah scans each page as he flips through the journal. It is the smallest of the books Heather loaned me. "There are no more entries from her. The next entry starts the journal of another, but there's no more mention of living reapers or the man at the church."

"What about Father Galen?"

Josiah shakes his head, putting the

book down. "My guess is that her conscience got the best of her, and she confessed to Bishop Whitmore, sealing her fate as well as Father Galen's."

"He killed them." Something niggles at the back of my mind, like an itch I can't scratch. Something about the name Whitmore.

"Yes, most likely."

"That's awful. They didn't do anything wrong. To burn someone alive to cleanse them…"

"The early days of the Church were barbaric. It wasn't about God, especially to some. It was about control and power. They committed crimes against humanity in the name of God. It was a dark time, but it is not the same today. You understand that, Mattie? The Church is better, aware of their past sins, and they work not to let power consume them."

"Are you Catholic?"

He smiles sheepishly. "Yes."

"Then maybe your ideals about the Church are a little biased?"

"Maybe, but I don't think so. It is not the same Church it once was. They do good now."

"And people like Bishop Whitmore don't exist?"

"I'm sure they do, but they are reined in better, and if discovered, the Church has its own methods of dealing with it."

"I guess."

"Can I ask you a question?" Josiah takes a sip of water. He's hesitant, which makes me curious.

"Sure."

"Do you believe in God?"

"Yeah."

"Why?" He cocks his head to the side. "After all you've been through, how can you believe?"

"You're not the first person to ask me that. Dan can't get it either."

"I know why I believe. I'm just curious as to your motivations. You went through some truly horrific events."

"Maybe that's precisely why I do believe. Because I knew that no matter what, someone was with me. It's hard to put into words, but I guess it comes down to faith that I wasn't alone through all those bad times. It gave me strength, let me fight for myself. I never waited on anyone to come to save me. I never will. My old Sunday school teacher told me God helps those who help themselves, and that's what I've always done."

It really is hard to put into words, at least ones that make sense. I can't explain why I believe. I just do. One of my foster homes took me to church. The feeling I got there was unlike any I've ever had before or since. It was as if someone hugged me when I walked across the threshold and has never let go. It was enough to convince a scared kid she wasn't alone, and it did give me strength. It got me through some tough times, not just the recent tragedies. It kept me sane.

"Anyway, enough about this." Josiah ruffles my hair, sensing my unease at discussing my religion. "Zeke tells me you managed to walk onto a different plane without realizing it."

I frown, not understanding what he's talking about.

"You were at the lake, I believe, and got lost from your friends?"

Ohhh, he means when I found Mason

and Paul's little serial killer burial ground. I'd gone to sleep, and when I woke up, I was alone. Everyone had left, or so I'd thought. In reality, I'd slipped onto a different plane, one that mirrored the one I was in. It also housed a very scary...something. What it was, I still don't know, but it scared the bejesus out of me, maybe a little more than even Silas does.

Zeke admitted to me that the Cranes used this ability to evade being caught in illegal activities. Knowing my family engages in criminal activity bothers me, but I also get the feeling they only do when it's necessary. From what I've observed, they run a very legitimate and lucrative business. Not one I want to try to learn, but still, it's good to know they aren't complete crooks.

"It was an accident. I didn't even know what I'd done until Zeke explained it to me."

"Once we get this sorted with the Fallen Angel, we'll start your lessons on how to traverse the different planes of existence. You need to be able to recognize when you've stepped into one."

"Some of them are dangerous?"

"Lethal," Josiah agreed. "You need to know where you are at all times."

One more thing to worry about if I survive the night.

The doorbell rings, and my gut twists. I know who it is, but I'm not sure I want to face him right now. Or ever.

But Fate has never been my friend, and he barrels into the kitchen, his eyes blazing with a white light, his mouth twisted in a feral snarl.

My very own Guardian Angel, Eli Malone.

Chapter Thirteen

We stare at each other, neither saying a word. Trepidation dances along my spine. The white light blazing in his eyes dims so their natural aqua color seeps back in. They're beautiful and have always fascinated me. His eyes should terrify me, especially since I know what his ancestors have done to the women they love.

I've been in those women's shoes, felt their emotions while the man they loved murdered them, thanks to my visions. And Eli might love me. I don't know. The Guardian Angel bond screwed everything up. I can never be sure if his feelings are real or there because he thinks that's what I need.

"What are you doing here?" I ask when I can't take his silence anymore.

"I had to make sure you were okay." He grimaces. "It kept eating away at me until Mom told me to get my butt over here and verify for myself you were fine."

It must have been really bad for his mother to say that. Heather warned us both to stay away from each other because of the curse he carries. She wouldn't send him to me lightly.

His hand starts to reach out, but then he drops it. Josiah clears his throat. "I'm going to be over there taking stock of the fridge." Getting up, he gives Eli a wide berth. It would be too much to expect him to leave us alone. He knows about the curse too. Eli is destined to murder the woman he falls in love with, and because of our bond, everyone is afraid it will trigger an emotion like true love and he'll come after me. Stupid curse.

"What happened?" He's abrupt, brusque. Not like him at all.

"Protection demon. Same one that showed up in New Orleans."

His lips thin. "Who wants you dead, Hilda?"

I shrug. At this point it could be any number of people or demons. Maybe even my MIA mother.

He rubs his eyes, the first signs of weariness starting to show now that his Guardian Angel juice is wearing off. He looks worn out. My first instinct is to hug him, but I know he'll go stiff as a board if I do. He doesn't want to be here.

"As you can see, I'm fine. You don't have to be here."

He frowns, shoving his hands in his pocket. It's something Dan does too, when he's nervous. "I know you're upset. I can feel it."

Danged bond.

"Of course, I'm upset. A demon attacked me in a house that is supposed to be demon-proofed, but it got in. I almost died, Eli."

He flinches. "I should have been there to protect you."

"No. You need to worry about Benny,

not me. I'm fine."

"You're always fine, aren't you, Hilda?" He worries his bottom lip. "Even when everyone around you is falling down, you always come out fine."

What am I supposed to say to that accusation? It's true. Everyone around me gets hurt, and I come out smelling like, well, not roses, but smelling better than the others.

"I'm sorry, Eli."

"You don't have anything to be sorry for, Emma Rose." Zeke walks into the kitchen. He must have been lurking in the hallway. "What happened to the boy isn't your fault."

"Then whose fault is it?" Eli shouts, his anger finally spilling over. "We wouldn't even be here if not for her!"

"Yes, you would. Your father investigates cases like this, and he'd have come to Charlotte whether you met my daughter or not. He would have gotten himself involved in the case. Taking the boy was not a slight to Emma Rose but to James himself. You can't blame that on her."

"Everything was fine until she showed up. Now it's all messed up."

It's my turn to flinch, and I see the emotion flicker in his eyes. He felt how deeply those words cut me. Eli closes his eyes and takes several deep breaths, trying to get his emotions under control.

"I'm sorry, Hilda. You didn't deserve that."

"No, I didn't." My own voice sounds small, wounded. I think I *do* have feelings for Eli, outside of the bond. Why else would his words hurt so much? "Go home, Eli."

He walks over and hauls me up out of the chair, wrapping his arms around me. Peace washes over me. Instant relief. The hurt, the anger, the blame all just melt away in his arms. As soon as he leaves, it'll flood back, but for a minute, it's nice to be calm and at ease.

"I'm sorry, Hilda." His breath tickles my ear, and I shudder. He always does this to me. "I'm messed up. Blaming you isn't right. I know that."

"But you do."

He lays his head on top of mine. "I'm

trying not to."

"Mattie!"

Dan. He lumbers into the kitchen, Caleb right behind him. The look on his face is enough to pull me out of Eli's embrace and straight into his. Whereas Eli gives me insta-calm, Dan's is deeper. His very presence eases every worry I have. I feel safe with him, even safer than with my own Guardian Angel.

"You're not hurt?" I tip my head up so I can look him over. I know he swore he wasn't, but I've been worried since he hung up on me.

"Nah, Squirt. I'm all good." He hugs me to him, pressing a kiss to my temple. The slow burn that only Dan can cause seeps into my skin and spreads outward. "Let's see it."

He wants to see my neck. I release him and pull my hair back. A shocked hiss escapes Eli, and he's standing right by Dan in a matter of seconds. Accusation rolls off him. "I thought you said you were fine."

"This is nothing. I've had worse."

"She has." Dan traces the deep red

mark with his finger, and a different kind of shiver rolls through me. Eli notices it, and his eyes narrow.

"True. The ghost at UNC did more damage." The first time I'd met Doc, a ghost attacked me where he was lecturing. Dan had been convinced I did it myself, and I'd stormed off, only to get nabbed by Mrs. Olson, the resident psycho.

"What happened?" Zeke pushes both of them out of the way. The fury dancing in his eyes when he sees the reddened skin is enough to make anyone cower, but I know it's not directed at me.

"Protection demon."

"That's not possible. The house is demon-proofed."

"Well, not for this one. It got in and almost killed me."

"How did you get away?" He looks up at his father, who nods and slips out of the room. What is Josiah up to?

"I didn't. It exploded and left this nasty black mess on the bed."

"It dissolved, not floated away into smoke?" His eyes burn brighter, the

146

anger deepening.

"Yeah."

"Dan killed it." Caleb draws our attention back to him while he tells Zeke about their theory of the one that showed up at his truck, and Zeke listens carefully. Caleb's body is tense, and he looks ready to jerk me away from Zeke. It's that whole Malone guardian thing. They were bred to protect living reapers, and to them, my dad is probably the biggest threat to me. But I know better.

"I've never heard of anything like that, but then again, I've never known a soul-bonded pair either."

"A whatsit?" Soul-bonded?

"Your soul is tied to Dan's, and his to yours. They are bonded. It's something only told of in legends and myths. No one believed it, but the two of you defy logic. It's quite possible the demon didn't understand what it smelled and simply came to investigate why he reeks of you."

Okay. Fifteen-bajillionth weird thing today.

"Now we just need to find out who sent it and make sure they are disposed of."

The threat is there in his voice, and I shiver. This is the man everyone told me about. The man who will hurt anyone in his way.

"It's already taken care of."

Zeke's shrewd eyes zero in on Dan. "Who was it?"

"It's taken care of. No more will be coming."

Zeke lets out a string of words I can only assume are curses. They're in French, so I can't say for sure. I'm betting he just remembered Dan can lie to him as easily as I can, or in this case, withhold all the evidence.

"Caleb, who sent the protection demon after my daughter?"

"Dan's mom." Caleb's eyes widen and he slaps a hand over his mouth much like I do when I blurt stuff out unintentionally around Dan.

"Your mother?" Zeke gets quiet—so quiet, it scares me. "Your *mother* tried to kill my daughter?"

"She understands that if she harms Mattie, she hurts me. She won't do anything else to hurt her. I promise."

"Do you think I care about her promise?" The enraged words tumble through stiff lips, and he stands, taller than any of the boys in the room. His eyes darken to a deep blue that looks like the midnight sky right before a storm. "She…"

I lay my hand on his arm. "Zeke, don't."

He glances down at me. "She tried to hurt you."

"Because she hates me." He knows Mrs. Richards was Claire's sister. She blames me for Mom's death. "It's okay. I accepted it a long time ago. But she was only trying to protect her son, the same way you would me if you thought it would keep me safe. You can't blame her for that."

His lips quiver. The argument is there on his tongue, but whatever he sees in my face softens his expression.

"Please don't hurt her."

"You would show mercy to someone who's never shown you a kindness?"

I nod. "She's his mom."

"You are truly special, Emma Rose. Do you know that?"

That's one way of putting it. I wouldn't call my freak show of a life special, though.

"What are you doing here, Eli?" Caleb is not so subtle in his attempt to get the conversation off Dan's mom. I appreciate it. Zeke could flip at any second. He never agreed not to hurt her. That didn't escape any of us.

"I couldn't get this feeling she's in danger out of my head. It was driving me nuts, and Mom ordered me to go get it out of my system."

"You left her alone?" Caleb is already yanking out his phone.

"No. I'm not stupid. Ava's with her."

"Is there any news?" Zeke leads me over to the table and pushes me in first, putting himself between me and the boys. He's going into overprotective mode.

Caleb shakes his head, looking as weary as Eli. "Nothing. It's like they disappeared into thin air."

"I have some calls in." Zeke thanks Mrs. Banks for the coffee she set down on the table. "If the boy is still in the city, we'll know by nightfall."

"How could you know that?" Eli frowns, but Zeke only stares back. It's one of those situations where it's better not to ask all the details.

"That's why we were on our way over here to begin with." Dan takes a seat across from me. "I was hoping you'd be up to testing our connection."

"You want me to try to see what you saw." It was something he'd asked me in the hospital, but I'd been so sick, Zeke threatened bodily harm. The seizures almost killed me. I'm not sure opening myself up to something else is a good idea. My body's having enough trouble handling my reaping abilities waking up. Not sure what it'll do if I try to sync up with Dan's.

"No. Absolutely. Not."

Frigid blue eyes bore into Dan's.

"Zeke…"

"No!" he shouts. "You almost died, Emma Rose. I will not let you do this. It might set your seizures off again."

"Neither Deleriel or Silas is going to

let me die before they get what they want from me."

"You don't know that."

"I do. They've both said so. If this can help find Benny, then I have to try."

"It could kill you." Fear coats every word.

"But I still have to try."

"None of this is your fault. The boy is blaming you, and you feel guilty for something you had no control over. Don't let it blind it you, *ma petite*. This could kill you."

"And it would be worth it to save his life. I know him, Zeke. I'll never forgive myself if I don't try. Besides, it probably won't even work."

"It will work, my darling girl, and that's precisely why I can't allow you to do it."

I barely have time to blink before Silas latches onto me, and then we're falling into darkness.

Chapter Fourteen

Silence.

When I wake up, silence is the only thing I hear. It's unbearable, really, like being in a vacuum devoid of sound. I should open my eyes, but then my situation will become real, and I want to imagine I'm still asleep in my bed and this is all only a nightmare. A horrible nightmare I can wake up from.

But it's not, and I know that.

I move my hands, and cold metal greets my fingertips.

I've only ever woken up on a cold metal table once before. Silas had given me a tattoo. He didn't trust Caleb not to screw it up. It allowed me to see what happened to a ghost without experiencing it firsthand. Something I realized I could do when all those girls who Mason and Paul murdered came to hunt me down. They blamed me, at least the ones Mason murdered. He always called them my name when he murdered them. It's unpleasant to experience death over and over.

Silas agreed. I think he did it to protect my sanity so I would be well enough to deal with Deleriel. I still don't know why he wants him dead, but he does. He created me for the sole purpose of destroying the Fallen Angel.

I'm lying face down on the table, and a cool breeze drifts over my very naked backside. I'm sore too. He has to have inked me again. I stretch and hiss in pain. My entire back is on fire, not just a single spot.

Humming sounds to my right, and I know it's him. He'd snatched me out of the kitchen. Zeke, Dan, and Eli have to be going insane. Especially the boys. They are bound to me. Cracking an eye, I can barely see him standing beside me, his usual tray of tools in front of him. I blink, trying to clear the bleariness from my eyes. I squint, and he starts to come into focus. He's loading up a tattoo needle with black ink from a small glass jar that pulses with a faint red hue.

Nope. I've had enough ink for one day. He's not getting near me with that thing. I prepare myself to roll over to escape, but he reaches out a hand, catching me by the hair.

"Be still, Emma Rose. I'm not done yet." He puts the jar down and takes the needle from the hand currently holding my hair in a death grip. "I will strap you down if I have to. I don't want to, but I will."

"What are you doing?"

"Trying to keep you alive." He's vexed, but I have every right to be mad. He'd kidnapped me and inked me again without my permission. The only thing that keeps me still is the trace of fear I hear shimmering in his voice.

"How is this going to keep me alive?"

"It's an ancient spell, but it's very

Apryl Baker

delicate. You need to be still. If I screw up one small detail, it won't work. You need to be absolutely still, do you understand?"

"But isn't it just the ink that's spelled?" That's what Heather had told me, anyway.

"Usually, but not in this instance. The tattoo design is just as important as the ink. Are you going to make me strap you down?"

"No." I can't abide being strapped down. Not since I was tortured while restrained, thanks to Mrs. Olson. Just the thought has my hands shaking. A tremor runs through me, and I can't shake the panic that creeps in.

"Good girl." Silas strokes my hair, and it calms me. It's the same thing Zeke did when I was in the hospital. It's comforting. "This is going to hurt, my darling girl, but you must not move an inch. Do you understand?"

I nod, and he moves away, picking the needle back up. He wipes a cold cloth across my back, and the smell of antiseptic tickles my nose. I hate the

156

smell. It's one I associate with hospitals, my least favorite place in the world.

I am not prepared for the first bite of the needle when it presses into my skin, and I hiss. All those idiots who tried to talk me into getting a tattoo said it wouldn't hurt, that it'd feel like the sting of a sweat bee. Liars. The lot of them.

This *hurts*!

"How is this going to help me?" I grit my teeth against the pain and fist both hands around the edge of the table on either side of me.

"Don't move!"

"Sorry, but it hurts!"

"I know." His voice softens, and some of the ire leaves it. "I thought you'd be out longer."

"How long have I been out?"

"A few days."

"Days?" I whisper, my mind seizing up. Mary…oh, God, Mary. Deleriel…

"Be at ease, Emma Rose. Time moves differently here. Don't panic. It's only been a few seconds on your plane."

A slow, grateful sigh leaves me. She's still safe. But the longer I'm here, the longer Benny is with that monster. I need to get back.

"Why did you yank me before I could do the sketch for Dan?"

"Because it would have worked."

"Then why stop me?"

"Because despite your gifts, you are body is still very much human and therefore fragile. Melding your mind with Daniel's would have turned it to mush. You would have seen everything, perhaps even managed to do the sketch, but you would have fried your brain doing it."

"Oh."

"Yes, oh." He tsks. "I told you once already, I'm not going to let you kill yourself before you do what you were made to do."

"But Benny…"

"The boy is perfectly safe."

"No, he's not. He's with that, that…monster."

Silas chuckles. "No, he's not. He's here."

"Here?" I swivel my head to look at him. "What do you mean, he's here?"

"I told you I would get the boy, and I

did. He wasn't any the worse for wear aside from a few bruises from being thrown into the trunk of the car. At the moment, he's asleep. He should stay that way until I decide to wake him up."

"Where are we?"

"In my home, of course."

"That doesn't tell me anything, Silas."

"We are in the innermost circle of hell."

Well, fudgepops.

He laughs at my expression. "You are safe here. No one can detect you or the boy for as long as you remain inside my wards."

"Is Mary here too?"

"Yes, but you cannot help her." He glares down at me. "I can see the wheels turning in that pretty head of yours, and you can forget it. She's encased in Deleriel's domain. There would be no saving either of us if we tried to get past his wards."

"I can't just leave her."

"Yes, you can."

Why is he so calm? Doesn't he understand what captivity will do to her?

I'm barely holding myself together at the mere mention of restraints. Mary had it worse than I did. I was only trapped for a few days. She was there weeks. Weeks. She has to be scared out of her mind. I can't just leave her there.

"Hush, child." He brushes my hair to the side to study his handiwork. "You'll save your sister by defeating Deleriel, and you can't do that if you don't let me finish this."

"What is this supposed to do? You never said."

"No, I didn't say." He shifts me so I'm at an angle on the table, but refuses to elaborate, which only irritates me more. Enough to get me past my fear of the demon who is my grandfather.

"Silas."

"Mattie."

He used my name. He never does that unless he's either really angry or losing his patience. His British accent has thickened as well. Never a good sign.

"Owww!" I can't stop the cry from slipping past my lips when the needle attacks the sensitive skin right behind my ear.

Silas grunts, but doesn't say anything else to me. He goes back to his work.

Hours.

Hours he's sat here and inked me without so much as a word. He shifts me every so often for better access, but other than that, there's nothing but the silence, the sound of my breathing, and the staccato of the needle gun.

Once he's done with my right side, he goes to the middle of my back and works his way up my spine around the other side of my head to the back of the other ear.

I'm not ashamed to say tears flowed. It hurt. Like thousands of bee stings that won't stop.

"You look like my sister."

Silas startles me so much I jump. Had he still had the needle against my skin, I would have ruined his design. He has a sister? I shouldn't be surprised. I guess I just didn't think demons had families. I mean, he is my grandfather, so it's not that big of a leap. Still, it's weird.

"Maybe that's why you're my favorite.

You remind me of her." He places bandages over my back and along my neck. "She was feisty, like you. Had a mouth on her too."

"Did she die?"

"No."

Okay. "Where is she, then?"

"Here."

"She lives here with you?"

"No."

One-word answers are not getting us anywhere.

"I don't understand. How can she be here, but *not* be here?"

He leans down and presses a kiss to my forehead. "I will tell you when you wake up. I have much to teach you and little time to do it, Emma Rose. Sleep, child." He whispers a sing-song phrase in that language I don't understand, and my eyes droop, blackness eating away my vision until I'm drifting away into nothingness.

***

The shrill beeping of an alarm disturbs

my sleep. I growl and roll over, trying to smack it off, but my hand hits empty air. Did Mary move my alarm clock again? She thinks it's funny to watch me stagger around half asleep hunting it down. I'm going to beat her.

Sitting up, I rub my eyes and yawn. "Mattie?"

I pause mid-rub and crack an eyelid. Benny is sitting cross-legged across from me, his aqua eyes round and terrified. He has a couple bruises on him, just like Silas said…Silas!

The reality of where I am comes crashing down on me. I'm in Hell. With Silas.

Anything you want.

I'd promised him anything if he'd get Benny back from Deleriel.

And here's Benny sitting across from me.

What do I owe the demon?

My soul?

But wouldn't it be better to give it to him than Deleriel?

I shake my head. Stupid. Silas has nefarious plans for me. I can feel it. His owning my soul would not be better or worse than Deleriel owning it.

"You okay?" I run my hands over him, checking for injuries. Aside from the bruises and a cut on his eye, he looks okay. Thank God.

"Yeah, but I'm scared."

"Me, too." I pull him into my lap and hug him. "It's going to be okay, though. I promise."

"There's a demon here." He does that loud whisper that only kids can. "I didn't know what to do. I saw him. Daddy says to run when I see one, so I did and found you, but you wouldn't wake up."

"I'm awake now." I ruffle his hair. "Silas won't hurt you, Benny. I won't let him."

"You know him?" He looks up, confused. "Demons are bad, Mattie. We have to get out of here."

"We can't, Benny. We're not home, we're on another plane of existence."

"Another what?"

How to explain it to a little kid when I don't quite understand it myself?

"We're a long, long way away from

home, and Silas is our bus ticket home. Until he's ready to take us, we're stuck."

"But…"

"No buts, kid. We have to deal with it. Silas won't hurt you, I promise."

"He's a demon!" Benny tugs at his hair, clearly aggravated. I have to get him to calm down before Silas's hounds hear him. I do not want to deal with Hell Hounds.

"So am I."

He stops mid-rant and stares at me, eyes as big as a house. "What?"

"It's true. Silas is my grandfather."

His mouth falls open. "No, you're not. You don't look like a demon, and you're nice."

"Thanks." I hug him again. "But that doesn't change anything. I am part demon, but that doesn't mean I'm evil or will ever do anything mean to you. Let me make you a deal."

"What kind of deal?" He cocks his head, trying to see some indication of my demon heritage, I think.

"If you trust me, I'll keep you safe. Deal?"

"Okay. Deal."

"And so it begins."

We turn to see Silas standing in the doorway grinning like a fool. His black eyes are shining with pride.

I close my own eyes and groan. He heard me make a deal with Benny. But it didn't mean anything. I was just trying to calm him down, but Silas isn't going to care about that. A deal's a deal to him, and I just made one. Freaking fantastic.

"You are supposed to be asleep." Silas walks into the room, carrying a tray of food. My stomach growls, and Benny scoots behind me, peeping at Silas.

"He woke up." I sniff, the scrumptious smell of cheese sandwiches and tomato soup invades my senses, and my mouth waters.

"I can see that." He sets the tray down on the bed in front of me. "There's enough there for both of you."

"Benny, this is Silas." I try to coax him out from behind me, but he clutches my back, and I hiss, the pain immediate.

Silas reaches behind me and grabs Benny by the scruff of the neck and hauls him up to eye level. "You hurt her."

"He didn't mean to." I try to keep my voice calm. No need to upset either of them, but I know that look in Silas's eyes. He's pissed.

"Do you think that matters?" Silas swings him like a pendulum and Benny whimpers. "The only person allowed to hurt you, my darling girl, is me."

"Silas, you can't hurt him. I promised to keep him safe."

"You promised, I didn't."

"How am I supposed to keep my word, then?"

His black gaze swivels back to me with a calculating gleam. "Well, now, that's a very good question, Emma Rose."

Crap on toast. Wrong question.

"What do you think will keep me from letting my pups chase him? They love to play, and he'd make a perfect chew toy. They're just barely weaned from their mother and have yet to be blooded."

"Silas, you harm one hair on his head…"

He grins. "Oh, no, my darling girl. If I do harm a hair on his head, it's going to be all *your* fault."

"My fault?"

"Mmhmm." He leans in and sniffs Benny. "Unless you do exactly as you're told, I will let my pups blood themselves on him. Do you understand the rules?"

I have no doubts he'd hurt Benny to make me obey him. "Perfectly."

He drops the kid back on the bed. "He stinks. Make sure you shower him before you come down to the studio. You remember where it is?"

I nod, not trusting myself not to snark at him. I want to seriously hurt him right now.

"Good girl."

He walks out, leaving me alone with a very scared little boy.

Chapter Fifteen

Once we've eaten and gotten cleaned up, I lead Benny down the dark hallway outside my bedroom to the studio. I do remember where it is. I've only been there twice, but it's not a place I'm likely to forget. Bad things happen there. Things I don't want Benny to see, but I can't leave him alone in my room either. One of Silas's hounds might find him, and he'd never even see it coming. Besides, he's terrified and clutching me like I'm the last lifeline in a sea of sharks.

The room is as I remember it, full of paintings, art supplies, and the metal table. It's empty. Thank God.

Silas is staring out a window I hadn't noticed. Does Hell even have a view? I clear my throat to announce our arrival, but he doesn't turn. "Why is the boy here?"

"Because he's scared."

"He'll be even more scared if he stays, Emma Rose." He finally turns and looks at me, the black talons that serve as his fingernails tapping his chin. "Do you really want him to see what happens in here?"

No, but I don't have a choice. I turn and get down on my knees in front of him. "Benny, I have to help Silas. He has to teach me how to defeat Deleriel. Do you know who that is?"

He nods, eyes solemn. "He...the man, he said he was going to feed me to Deleriel, but he would have fun first." The little boy shivers. "He was going to hurt me."

"Yes, he was." I want to hug him, but he needs to understand. "I have to do bad things so I can stop him. It's going to scare you, but no one will hurt you. I promise."

"Bad things?" he whispers, his gaze darting to Silas.

"Yes. I don't want to do them, but I have to. Do you understand?"

He nods again. "Papa sometimes has to do bad things to save people."

"It might make you afraid of me, Benny, but I promise, I will never hurt you."

"I know." He lays his little hand against my cheek. "I trust you, Mattie, even if you're a demon."

"As touching as this Hallmark moment is, we need to get busy." Silas strides across the room and opens a door. I hear cries of pain, the clinking of chains. Benny does not need to see this. Looking around, I find paper and colored artist pens. I set him up in the farthest corner with his back to the room.

"No matter what you hear, you do not look. Just keep drawing pictures. Promise me."

"I promise." He picks up a piece of paper and starts to draw. I wish I had headphones for him, but there's nothing else I can do to protect him from God only knows what Silas has planned.

"Come, Emma Rose. My patience is growing thin."

I cast one last look at Benny and then walk over to Silas. The room he's looking into makes me want to throw up. Bile rises in my throat, but I force it down. He has a plethora of racks, some standing, some made from tables. The place stinks of death, blood, and pain.

"Sometimes people do not want to pay up when their notes come due." He walks into the room and I follow him, trying not to touch any of the bloody surfaces. "It's not that we want to cause them pain, but when they try to welsh on a deal, there are consequences."

He stops near the back of the room, and the woman he has suspended on the wall, held there by hooks in her flesh, begs me to help her. Her fear is palpable.

"This is Jemma. I met her ten years ago when she was just a groupie, going from one band to the next. All she wanted was to sing. She does have a semi-decent voice. Nothing like yours, but she's good."

How does Silas know I can sing?

"So, what, she made a deal to become famous in exchange for her soul?"

"If only it were that simple."

Uh oh.

"You see, Emma Rose, I don't make deals with innocents. Not my style. Our Jemma here was jealous. She managed to snag a spot as a backup singer right before I met her. She was working with a small girl band called Dangerous Gypsies. They were popular in Ireland. Jemma wasn't content to wait and work her way up. Oh, no. She wanted what Hannah had."

"Hannah?"

"The lead singer." Silas swipes a clawed finger down Jemma's cheek, drawing blood and flesh. It's a sensation I distinctly remember, as he'd done something like that to me not so long ago. "Jemma wanted to be the lead singer. So, she summoned a crossroads demon."

"You."

"Ireland isn't one of my usual haunts. I just happened to be in the area. She wanted Hannah dead. Not out of the picture or injured so she couldn't sing anymore, but dead. She wanted no chances of her coming back to the band. She'd do anything, she said."

Anything you want.

Words I'd uttered myself.

"You see, most people want the most boring and mundane things. Jemma here suffered from greed and lust. She wanted what someone else had. Her story isn't unique. It's dull, but it's a common one. She gave away her soul to get what she wanted. What's a soul compared to ten years of fame and fortune? They always think this, until it comes time to pay the piper. Deals must be honored."

"Please." Jemma turned her tortured face to me. "Please help me. I'll do anything if you help me."

Her pleas eat at me. I'm hardwired to help ghosts, and it is her soul pleading with me. She may be here in the flesh, but I can see her soul. It's bleeding and in pain. I reach out, but Silas smacks my hands.

"No." He steps in front of me. "This

soul is mine. You cannot help her. Keep those instincts in check."

"How do you expect me to do that?" I peek around him, and her soul tugs at me.

"You either keep them in check or my pups get a new toy. Your choice."

Dang it!

Silas smiles and starts unhooking her from the wall. She screams when her flesh tears as he removes her from the rack. I swallow the bile. I will not puke.

"Do you know why I put her here?"

"No." My voice is so low I barely hear myself.

"It's in her contract. Standard clause. She runs, and she bleeds." Silas throws her over his shoulder and motions me to follow him back outside. I shoot a glance Benny's way, but he's got his back turned, coloring. *Please, kid, please don't look.*

He lays her down on the steel table, gleaming in the light. Her eyes are wild and she looks everywhere, searching for an escape, but there is none to be had. I ache to help her, but the quiet humming coming from the corner stays my hand. I promised to protect him. He's innocent.

"Had she not run, my hounds would have done their work. Her soul would be in its cage, and her physical body would have remained behind. Because she tried to get out of her deal, she must suffer. All in the contract. The devil's in the details. Remember that, Emma Rose. Contracts have to be adhered to. Verbal or written. It's imperative. Our word is our bond."

"I'm not making any deals with anyone, Silas."

He chuckles. "You already have."

"I have not. I was just trying to keep Benny from…"

He laughs. "Have you already forgotten the deal you made with me, Mattie Louise Hathaway?"

"No."

He smiles, his teeth lengthening just a bit until they look more like a mouth full of vampire fangs. "I fulfilled my part of the bargain. The boy is safe. You have yet to do the same."

"What do you want?"

"A favor."

"A favor?" I draw the word out, not

knowing where he's going with this.

"Yes. When I call and ask for a favor, you will grant it, no matter the cost to you."

"You don't want my soul?"

"No. You have to have your soul intact to be able to give it to Deleriel, or at least make him *think* you're going to give it to him."

Silas turns and starts collecting his canning jars. The glass is clean, at least. "Grab my brushes for me, please."

The old mason jar that houses his brushes sits on a shelf of an antique display piece. The worn stone is smooth to the touch, and a little spark of electricity shoots up my arm when I pick it up. It's not an unpleasant sensation, more like a welcoming stroke against my skin. Power brushes along my fingers, ghosting along my arm. These brushes hold life and death. Much like my reaping abilities. It's familiar to me.

"Do you feel it, Emma Rose?" He leans closer, his eyes hooded. "Can you feel the power of what you are about to do?"

"What am I about to do?" I can't move, frozen, streams of power washing through me. It's heady.

"You're going to pull a soul from its body and put it into a painting."

"What? No."

"*Yes*." He takes the brushes before I drop the jar. "You have to keep those reaping abilities buried. This will go against everything you are, but you have to know how to do it. It is the only way to trap Deleriel."

"Trap him?"

"You cannot kill an Archangel, Mattie. You can only trap them. You have to be able to pull his soul into the picture. Once he's trapped, we can release all the tortured souls he's captured over the centuries."

I cock my head, thinking. Trapped souls...

"He has your sister."

He doesn't look at me, and I know I'm right.

"You went to all this trouble to save her."

"I am what I am because of her." He

gives me a jar and a small knife. "You need to bleed her."

"I don't think I can do that, Silas."

His hands wrap around my neck in a blink of an eye. "Yes, Emma Rose, you can, and you will. You do want to keep the boy safe."

"Of course, I do, but…"

Claws sink into my throat, piercing the skin. I feel the warm trickle of blood almost as soon as the pain from his claws. "Do not test me, Emma Rose. We are too close to winning to let your conscience get the best of you now. I will not allow it. If that means I have to flay the flesh from the boy, I will, and then I will put him on the rack and let him suffer. Is that what you want?"

I feel the blood drain from my face. The truth is staring me in the eye. He won't let anyone or anything stand in his way, including me. He will hurt Benny and force me to watch him do it. He's crazy.

And he terrifies me enough to make me do anything. "Okay. Tell me what to do."

"Good girl." He releases me, and I follow him over to Jemma, who looks as terrified as I feel. "You need to drain enough blood to paint with. Take her arm and slice her wrist lengthwise along the vein so she'll bleed out. Cutting across the wrist does nothing. The wound will barely bleed, clot, and close up."

"I'm so sorry." I pick up her arm and slice it as Silas instructed. I do it fast so as not to lose my nerve. She screams, and I turn my head to watch Benny. He stiffens, but he doesn't look. Good boy. I let her arm hang off the table, placing the jar directly under her hand. Rivulets of red stream down her fingers and drip into the jar, slowly filling it up.

"See, that wasn't so hard, was it?"

I ball up my fist to keep from hitting him. It was hard. I'm basically stealing her life away from her, trapping her soul, and every instinct I have is screaming at me to stop, to save her.

"It will get easier. I promise."

That's what I'm afraid of.

"What's going on here?"

My head swivels to see Kane, my

reaper trainer, staring at us like we've lost our minds. He looks from me to Silas to Jemma, and his face drains of blood.

"How did you get in here?" Silas stalks toward Kane, anger vibrating with each step.

"Silas, don't touch him!" I'm right behind him, grabbing onto him before he can get his hands on Kane. Not sure he can do anything to him, but I don't want to chance it.

"He can't hurt me." Kane's green eyes bore into me. "What are you doing?"

Silas tries to grab hold of Kane, but his arm goes right through him. He purses his lips, not happy.

"Learning how to trap a soul." No point in lying to him.

"You can't." He looks so horrified, I almost take the words back. Repulsion soon replaces the look of horror.

"I have to." Miserable, I look down at my feet, feeling as repulsed at myself as he is. "It's the only way to stop Deleriel. I can't kill him, but I can trap him."

"But to trap an innocent soul." Kane shakes his head. "It's…"

"Demonic?" Silas grins at him, enjoying his pain.

Kane's gaze turns to ice, and I shiver. He looks as dangerous as either Dan or Eli right now. I had no clue reapers could get that look. "You're asking her to commit a crime against her very nature. Do you know the damage it's going to do to her soul? It may never recover."

"Do you want her soul consumed by Deleriel?" Silas's expression hardens. "He'll gain all her abilities, and then he'll be able to come and go between the planes as he chooses. Not just Hell or Earth, but *anywhere*. I think your bosses and their bosses will overlook this small lesson in her education."

"I'm not talking about them." Kane tugs at his t-shirt. It's the same one he always wears. "I'm talking about Mattie. She will forever carry this on her soul. It'll never be whole again. You're going to break her."

"Do you know another way?" I ask wearily. "You want his children loose on humanity, on the souls in Heaven? Do you?"

"No."

"Then this is our only option, Kane."

"It's going to break you."

"I'm already broken." I shrug. "What's one more tear in my soul if it will save the people I love?"

"You're not broken, though, Mattie. Your light shines brighter than anyone I've ever met. It's why ghosts flock to you. Your light shines like the light of Heaven itself. If you do this, you're going to dim that light, maybe even snuff it out."

"So? If that means fewer ghosts 'flock to me,' as you put it, then that's a good thing. I'm tired, Kane, tired of being the Ghost Girl, of being the eye of the storm and having everyone around me fall to the winds I cause. I'm tired."

"You want to end up as a shade? Is that it? This is how you become those things we protect souls from in the Between. Is that what you want?"

It's what I deserve. I've caused so much pain to those I love. If this is my punishment, I will take it, and take it gladly. If it saves the people I love, I will accept it.

"And Dan?" Kane stalks towards me. "What about him? His soul is tied to yours."

"I'm trusting you to make sure he gets to where he needs to be. Besides, *this* isn't going to kill me. I may not live past tonight, but for right now, he's safe."

"Please don't do this." Kane twists his fingers, scrambling to come up with an argument to stop me, but he made up my mind for me. Deleriel and his children can't be set loose. And Kane will save Dan from the Between or my own fate. I trust him to do that.

"Let's get started."

Chapter Sixteen

Kane is pissed, but too bad. He's already told me as soon as I deal with Deleriel, the others are going to smite me down or something. So, what do I care if I have to suffer? Not the first time and probably not the last time it's happened. Dan does worry me, despite my bravado. I'm trusting Kane to keep him safe. If there's a way, the reaper will find it.

I thought he'd leave when I refused to listen to him. He's standing sullenly off to the side. I'd asked him to take Benny home, but he's a shade down here. Just a ghost of who he is. It's the only way he can travel to this plane. He'd need to be whole to take Benny home.

The glass jar still isn't full enough to switch out for another one. I check on Benny again to make sure he's okay. He looks a little white, but he's not flipping out. He didn't see anything, but he heard it. Nothing I can do about that either. The kid's tougher than he looks, though.

Silas is busy taking stock of his supplies. He has paints of all varieties and textures. If I weren't so angry, I might even be over there ogling them. Art supplies have always been hard for me to come by. Even with the Crosses. I never really asked Mrs. Cross for them. Not because she wouldn't get them, but because they are so expensive. She took me in, and I try my best not to be a burden to her.

Not that it stopped me from wrecking her life. It's my fault Mary is in danger this time. Deleriel took her to get to me. All I can do now is try to make it right.

Jemma keeps making these pleading sounds. I almost managed to drown it out earlier, but it keeps beating at this need to protect her soul. Kane says that's my instincts trying to urge me to do the right thing and save her. I can't, though. If I don't learn this, none of the people I care about will be safe.

It would be so much easier to be the Mattie of a year ago. The one who didn't care about anyone but herself. I would have run and left Mary and Benny to fend for themselves. I don't particularly like that girl, but she never had the worry I do now. She did what she wanted, and the heck to everyone else.

I want her back some days.

Like right now. If Silas forced her to do this, she would have with no qualms. That was the person I used to be. One who did what was best for Mattie Hathaway and *only* Mattie Hathaway.

I wander over to where Jemma is lying prone on the table, her life's blood slowly dripping out of her. The hopelessness in her expression makes me want to hide the shame in my own. This is wrong. No matter how I try to justify it, it's wrong. But what am I supposed to do? If I don't do this, God only knows what Deleriel might do to Mary.

Thoughts of being locked up in the dark haunt me the more I think about my sister. She spent weeks in the dark, a blindfold over her eyes, never knowing when the next moment of torment would strike. I can't sit and do nothing. Mary and I may not be blood sisters, but family isn't about whose blood runs in your veins. It's about the people who love you and who you love in return. We chose each other, and I'm not going to let her down.

Even if it means I blacken my own soul in the process.

"What do you see?" Silas's whispered words makes me jump. I hate how quiet he can be sometimes.

"A woman lying on a cold metal table bleeding to death." I can't keep the snarkiness out of my tone. Silas scares me, and when I'm scared, I get snarky. Can't help it.

"Don't make me hurt you, Emma Rose. It upsets me when I have to."

My face pulses exactly where he'd torn a strip of flesh from it. It's a memory that stays with me and not a feeling I'll ever forget. I have no doubts he'll do that and more if I refuse to obey him.

Turning my attention to Jemma, I study her. She's pretty. Late twenties, maybe early thirties. Dark blonde hair and expressive blue eyes. I can see her as a lead singer of a band.

"Look deeper." Silas pushes me closer to the table. "Look for what's beneath the mask."

Beneath the mask. It has to be what happened with Zeke earlier. I don't know how to mimic it again. Right now, she just looks like someone who's terrified out of her mind. I can't get past her fear. It's all I can sense, and it's driving my reaping skills to near madness.

Maybe if I touch her? But what happens if I can't control my need to help her? Silas will be pissed and might do me or Benny some serious damage, that's what.

Still, I have to try.

Gently, I lay my hand on her cheek, and she whimpers. The light inside of me, the one I associate with my reaping ability, swells up and reaches for her, but

I beat it back. It flinches, hurt that it can't do what it's meant to do. A small cry leaves me when the pain of denying my ability lashes through me. It feels like I got hit by the tail of a dragon that wrapped around my body and battered me.

Ignoring the pain, I concentrate on Jemma. Her eyes hold mine, and I let the world around me drift away, focusing on the depth of pain I see reflected in her baby blues. The longer I stare, the more I begin to discern other emotions reflected there. Fear is prevalent, but it's not the same fear you'd find for someone about to die. I've seen that before. This fear is because she knows she's going to pay for her crimes. She ran when her contract came due. That's what Silas said. I lean forward, pressing my fingers into her skin, and images start to flash across my vision.

Her as a teenager, going from concert to concert, following a band just as Silas said. I see her strike up a conversation with a girl holding a guitar, smiling and feeling awed the singer would even speak to her. I watch them become friends, and the women even offers her a position as a backup singer. Then I see the jealousy start to grow, the resentment and the anger. She wanted what she hadn't worked for. The other members of the band knew her, knew she could sing just as well as the lead singer, who was getting older. It should be Jemma up there on that stage.

Her grandmother once told her of a type of demon who would do anything for a price. She wanted fame, so she set out to do exactly what her grandmother warned her against.

I watch, repulsed as she summons a demon, her intent to become the new lead singer of the band. Much to my chagrin, I watch Silas question her, try to talk her out of her decision. She's so consumed by greed, jealousy, and hate there is no talking her down. She wants the girl dead and her own fame to happen overnight, no matter the price.

The younger version of her had no idea what it meant to give up her soul. It wasn't something tangible, something she could see or feel. She gave it away freely, and Silas took it, warning her she would have ten years of fame, and then it would be over. She would hand over her soul to him. She agreed.

The next day, the lead singer was pronounced dead, and she laughed with glee. In front of others, she pretended to be sad and grieving over the loss of her friend. She agreed to step in and help the band when they did a tribute concert in Dublin for their lost band member. That was the beginning of everything. She was brought on as the new lead singer, and she became the success she dreamed of.

She amassed wealth and fame over the years, but the older she got, the more she began to worry about her deal. What it meant. She started to research the subject, and what she found frightened her so much she began to find ways to protect herself for when the demon returned to collect payment.

Only there is no way to protect yourself from a contract with a crossroads demon. She made a deal, and that deal would be honored. She ran, but

Silas found her and dragged her here.

Through it all, she felt no shame at what she'd done. Her only regret was that she wasn't able to outrun the demon. I place my other hand over her heart and let that pulsing light on the edge of my vision fill me up and spread outward into the woman.

The blackness of her soul makes me want to pull away, but I don't. I look hard, searching for something, anything that would give me a sign this woman has any goodness in her, but there is none. She's furious. Rage beats at her. All because she got what she wanted, but had to pay for it. There's nothing here but evil.

"Good girl." Silas hands me a brush and gently turns me to the canvas. "Now show us what you saw. Let each brushstroke draw some of the darkness out of her and onto the page."

Her image is burned into my mind. The fear, the pain, the hate. It's all there, eating away at me, and if I don't get it away from me, it'll consume me. Silas is a painter. I'm not.

Frowning, I glance around for paper and drawing tools. Realizing what I'm searching for, he hands me a giant sketchpad and charcoal pencils. I shake my head, trying to stop the pounding headache I know is caused by what I saw. I have to get it out.

Silas leads me to a chair, and I sit, ignoring the hardness of the surface, and start to draw. Each line pulls some of the hate from me and bleeds onto the page. The glass jar of blood sits next to me, and every so often, I dip my pencil into it. The page soaks up the blood like a sponge craves water. It spreads to every line of the drawing, enhancing it.

I purge what I took inside of me onto the paper, and when I finally look up hours later, Benny is watching me, a curious look on his face. Even Kane seems fascinated, despite his disgust.

"What?" I ask them both, stretching my fingers.

"Your eyes." Benny cocks his head. "They're yellow."

Yellow? Like the creepy kids?

"No, not yellow." Kane walks up to

me, his fingers tilting my face up to him. "They're gold. I thought they were yellow at first too, but it's the golden flakes in your hazel color. Black has replaced all the white and the iris is gold. Your eyes are glowing, Mattie." He leans in for a better look. "They're beautiful."

Silas squats beside me and focuses on the drawing instead of my eyes. His satisfied expression makes my skin crawl. I pull out of Kane's grip and look down. The portrait is gorgeous. Every emotion Jemma felt is reflected in the drawing. Her eyes plead for help, even while hate glows out of them.

"Now, seal the deal, Emma Rose." Silas pricks my finger. Blood wells to the surface. I dip my pencil into the droplet and sketch just a bit more detail into the shading of her eyes. The page flutters, breathing a sigh when my blood hits it. The effects of the image are immediate. It comes to life.

A slow hiss emanates from Kane. I refuse to look at him and see the disgust he must feel for me. I like Kane, despite his cowardly tendencies. I respect him.

His opinion matters to me.

"You did it, my darling girl!" Silas picks me up and swings me around. "I don't know how you unlocked your abilities, but you did it."

"I don't know how either." I take several deep breaths when he stops swinging me. It made me a little dizzy. "It happened earlier with Zeke."

"Your father?" Silas peers at me curiously. "What did you see?"

"What he's been trying to tell me since we met." I should never have let anyone plant seeds of doubt about his intentions toward me.

"And what is that?"

"That he'll never hurt me. He'd rather harm himself than me."

"Good to know." Silas grins. "Good to know."

"You will not hurt him, Silas." Rage springs up so fast, it scares me. "You will not touch a hair on the heads of anyone I love. Do you understand me?"

"Easy, little demon." Silas takes several steps away from me. "I have no plans for your father."

I'm not sure he means it, but I do know if he hurts him, Silas will die. Even if it's the last thing I do. He will suffer for hurting my family.

"What ability did she unlock?" Kane asks. I'm betting he's changing the subject to keep me from attempting to hurt Silas. It might not bode well for me if I do. He can hurt me in ways I can't even imagine, but this rage drives me to do things I normally wouldn't.

"The ability that will allow her to defeat Deleriel." He rubs his hands together gleefully. "I am so proud of you, Emma Rose."

"Yes, but what ability is that?" Kane presses, and I'm forced to reevaluate my earlier thought. He wasn't trying to distract Silas. He's curious…and a little afraid.

"The ability of Creation."

"Say what?" What's he talking about?

"Your reaping side gives you dominion over death. Your demonic side gives you the gift of manipulation and great power. Creation gives you dominion over life. It lets you see all there was, all there is, and all there will be. When you saw beneath Jemma's mask of humanity, you saw everything she was, she is, or she'll be. What did you see?"

"Evil."

Silas nods. "Yes, it's what I saw when I made the deal. It's the only reason I made that deal. I don't deal in innocents, only those who deserve the fates they sign on for."

Wow. I never knew Silas had any kind of conscience, but apparently, he does.

"Wait a minute. My blood was bringing images to life before…"

"Yes." Silas ruffles my hair affectionately. "That's how I knew you had inherited the ability. You just hadn't unlocked it all. Whatever served to do it, you now possess everything you need in order to trap Deleriel."

What unlocked it? I think back, and my eyes widen. "It was Deleriel!"

"What?" Silas asks, his expression turning to one of horrified fear. "What do you mean?"

"He came to me in the hospital. I forgot to tell you with everything going on with Mary and Benny. He healed me so I wouldn't die before he got my soul. When he did, I saw everything, right down to every molecule. That's when this started."

"Did he notice?" Silas grips my arms and shakes me. "Did he say anything?"

"Yes." I swallow past the lump in my throat. "He asked me what sort of blasphemy this was, and I'd better have answers for him tonight."

Silas releases me and starts to pace, muttering in that language I don't understand.

Benny tugs on my shirt. "He looks scared, Mattie."

"I know." Silas looks more than scared, he looks ready to run. My first instinct in any situation I can't control. Perhaps that's another trait I inherited from my demonic grandfather.

"Mattie."

The hushed awe in Kane's tone whips my head around to stare at him. He looks almost reverent. "What?"

"Do you know what you are?"

"No, but I know what I want to be.

Normal, no special skills or abilities. I just want a freaking *normal* life."

"Mattie, you hold power over life and death with the ability to manipulate it. That's…that's the ability of a god."

"No." I will not believe that.

"Yes." Silas stops pacing. "What Deleriel sought could not be created from humans, even human hybrids. Only a god could do what he wanted. Your mother was an ancient goddess from a different plane of existence. I was sworn to silence, as only you could unlock what you are. It was a promise I made to your mother, but now that you have discovered it, I can speak freely about it."

"No." My faith teaches that there is only one God, I won't listen to this nonsense.

Silas sighs. "Child, you can keep your religion close, but it still doesn't change the facts. You were created from a father who is part demon, part reaper. Your mother is part demon and your metaphysical mother is a goddess with the gift of creation. You can ignore it the rest of your life if you want, but to save yourself, your sister, and all the people you love, you're going to have to accept your heritage."

Lies. Lies. Lies. I sink down to my knees. It's all a lie.

Or a really bad nightmare I can't wake up from.

"Mattie." Kane lays a hand on my shoulder. "I know this is overwhelming, but the demon is right about one thing. Who you are doesn't change anything when it comes to your faith. You believe in God, and He believes in you. It's as simple as that."

"But...but if what Silas says is true, doesn't that mean I have to acknowledge there is another god or goddess in this situation?"

"You're taking those teachings literally." He smiles, and for the first time since he's shown up, he's not looking like he wants to puke. He looks calm and at peace. "It never states there aren't other gods out there, only that you will follow Him and Him alone. That's all. Don't let yourself get mired down in the literal interpretations of the Bible. It's not always as black and white as we try to make it. You can acknowledge your mother and still believe in God. He knows your heart and is not going to hold it against you."

"You think?" He looks sincere. Hope flutters to life in my chest. Maybe I can do this and not trash my faith.

"I do." He helps me to my feet. "The demon is right. Your faith is what defines you and your relationship with God. Not who birthed you."

Silas rolls his eyes. "Yes, yes. Now, let's see you pull the soul back out of the drawing."

"Uh, how do I do that?"

"The same way you absorbed the ghost in New Orleans. Only you want to hold her soul in your hand like a baby bird."

"And why do I need to do this?" He wants the soul trapped, and now he wants it released? He needs to make up his mind.

"Because, my darling girl, you need to understand the cycle of life and death. The next cycle is judgement. The soul needs to be judged and delivered on to its fate."

"Hold up. She signed a contract for her soul. Doesn't that mean it belongs to you?"

"Yes, but in order to prepare you for the biggest fight of your life, I'm prepared to let the young reaper here take her to be judged. You will accompany him into the Between and beyond. You must see and understand the cycle. It will hopefully grant you an insight that will give you an edge over Deleriel. He doesn't understand why it's important."

"What about Benny?"

"He's perfectly safe here with me."

"He'd be safer at home."

"You can take him when we're done here. Not until."

He's being stubborn, and there's no way he'll let me take Benny home. "What if you have to go out? What happens if something wanders in and finds him?"

Silas purses his lips and whistles. We all hear the click of nails across the wooden floor, but we can't see the Hell Hound. "This is Damien. He'll protect the boy."

"Why can't I see him?" Benny is looking exactly where the clicking stopped. "Is he too ugly to look at?"

Silas laughs. "No, boy. Hell Hounds aren't the monstrous beasts most believe. They are large, but they look more like a mix between a Lab and a Rottweiler. They are even more vicious than they appear in books and TV, though."

"Can I see him?" Benny gets down on his knees and eyeballs the empty space.

"You want to see him?" Silas asks, perplexed. "Why?"

"Because I like dogs."

That pulls a laugh out of the demon. "So do I, young one, so do I." He lays a hand on Benny's, and a wash of power radiates outward.

"Wow." Benny reaches out a hand and giggles. "He's not ugly at all."

Silas shakes his head. "Damien, protect the boy. Let no harm come to him."

A sharp bark sounds, and Benny strokes thin air. At least he's got someone to keep him company, as well as a protector. The Hell Hound will obey

Silas, and it's one worry off my shoulders.

"I think my hound is going to be useless after this." Silas sighs. "Now, let's finish today's lesson, shall we?"

Picking up my sketchpad from where it'd fallen, I look at the image. It's not hard to see the soul trapped there thanks to my reaping abilities. They call out to me to right the wrong I had done the soul. Reapers don't care if the person is good or bad, young or old. Our job is to ferry them through the Between to the other side, where judgement waits.

The soul is afraid, and I reach out with the soft light of my reaping gift and stroke the poor thing, trying to assure it all will be well. It sidles up to the warmth of the light and sighs, sensing something is here to help it. It only takes a little coaxing on my part to convince it to follow the light. We all watch as the mangled soul emerges from the page and hovers above it. I reach out and gather it in the palm of my hand. It's a tattered mess, tears and streaks of black all through it. Nothing I did damaged it.

Jemma damaged her own soul in life, and this is what is left of it.

"Very good, Emma Rose. You do please me." Silas reaches out and strokes the soul, but it shudders away from him. Black whiffs of energy roll off it, anger and rage the only emotion it can manage. It hates him. "Now, the two of you get a move on. Return the soul to be judged, and then I want you back here."

"How am I supposed to return?" I hold the little glowing ball close to my body to protect it. "Josiah said our family can't travel to this plane."

"No, they can't. You're different, though. You can get back here. All you have to do is imagine this room with me and the boy in it, and the way will open."

I frown, not wanting to leave Benny behind, but he can't go with us to the Between. I'm not even supposed to be there.

"The boy is fine. Now, go, Mattie Louise Hathaway, before I change my mind about keeping him safe. Damien may be blooded, but the pups aren't."

Crap on toast. I'd forgotten his earlier

threat. He'll do it if it means he gets what he wants. "Let's go, Kane."

Time to travel the Between.

Chapter Seventeen

The Between is the place between this world and the plane where souls go to be judged. Although the whole being judged aspect is new to me. I just thought they crossed over and went wherever they were supposed to go, be it Heaven or Hell. It makes me wonder how I'll be judged, especially after trapping a soul.

It's easy to open. I've done it so much all I have to do is think about it, and it opens. It reminds me of a snowy, static-y channel you see sometimes on TV late at night. The blank wall in Silas's studio bleeds to that snowy substance, and Kane gasps.

"How can you do that?" He shakes his head. "You should only be able to open a crack at best, not an entire wall."

"I don't know. It gets easier the more I do it." I rub my forehead, a headache starting right behind my eyes, which worries me. Using my abilities is what caused me to start having seizures to begin with, and now I don't have a choice in the matter. I have to use them or die tonight. Or whenever we technically leave. Silas promised when we go home, only a minute or so will have passed.

"Your skills are growing at a rapid pace." Kane looks worried, but I can't let his worry aggravate my own. If this kills me, it kills me. As long as I can save Mary and make sure Dan will be okay, then I'm good. After all the trouble I've caused the people I love, this is my Karma coming to bite me in the butt.

"I'm fine, Kane. Deleriel healed me, remember?" I hold back a wince when a rather nasty flash of pain rockets through my head. Not good, not good, not good. "Let's get this done. I don't want Benny alone with Silas for long."

I don't wait for an answer, I just walk into the snowy landscape. The last time I was here, the only thing I could see was a blank white landscape. Not this time. I see the forest, hear the things moving through the trees around me. We're definitely not alone.

The shades that live here survive by devouring lost souls. Sometimes a soul will break free from a reaper, trying to go back to the plane of the living, or they'll find their way here without a guide. They don't last long. I'd seen a shade once, felt it when it passed by my hospital room. I think it wanted to eat me. Thankfully, someone came along and scared it off, but it's an experience I'll never forget.

The soul in my hand quakes as we walk, able to sense the malevolent creatures around us. I pull it closer and try to comfort it. Not sure that's possible. The glowing red eyes peering at me from the underbrush are enough to make me weak, but I press on, refusing to let them see my fear.

Kane chuckles. "You don't even need

me to walk you through the Between anymore. The beasts are keeping their distance. You frighten them."

"Ha. They terrify me."

"I'm worried about you, Mattie. Don't think I don't know you're in pain. Your body isn't built to handle the full arsenal of skills a reaper has, let alone a demon or a god."

"Can we not talk about that, please?" It still makes me nervous thinking about my mother. "Let's discuss the powers that be trying to smite me instead."

He lets out a sigh. "At least I know why they want you dead once you take care of Deleriel. You pose a threat."

"A threat? How's that?"

"To their authority. You already flaunted the rules in their faces when you saved Dan from death. People who weren't supposed to die did…"

"If you're talking about Meg, I'd rather have her die quickly like that than in pain and humiliation any day of the week. You know Paul would have taken her, and I don't even want to think about what he would have done to her."

"Meg is one example, yes, but others died too soon, as will more. You cut the cords that bound you and Dan to the wheel of fate."

"I get how that might be relevant to Dan, but how am I not tied to it anymore?"

"Your and Dan's souls are bound together. What happens to one, happens to the other. When Dan's string was cut, so was yours. Neither of you should be here."

"Not my fault." Well, it is, but I am going to deny it to my dying breath. "So, are they going to smite me or what?"

"They're going to do *something*. I just don't know what. I've been driving myself nuts trying to figure out their plans so I can help you."

"Don't…" I stop and listen. Something's not right. It's too quiet. I put a finger to my lips to warn Kane and take in my surroundings. The place is empty. The shades have fled. What could scare the boogeyman?

"Do you feel that?" Kane whispers, stepping closer to me. "It's getting colder."

He's right. The Between is cold to begin with, but the temperature has dropped to single digits, maybe even into the negatives. It's enough to make my teeth chatter. The Between is full of ghost energy to begin with, so what kind of ghost can cause the deep freeze effect?

"There." Kane points to the left, and I squint, trying to see through the dense trees. Yellow, glowing orbs stare at me. Curious. Hungry.

I know those eyes.

They are the eyes of Deleriel's children.

Fudgepops.

It steps out of the shadows and shuffles closer to us, sniffing. It was once a little girl, maybe eight or nine. Dark hair is matted to her scalp, her fingers bent at odd angles. Bruises cover one side of her face, giving it a patchwork look. The bruises crisscross, making me think some kind of object caused them. Her dress might have been blue once, but it's stained brown in so many places, it's hard to tell. Dried blood. She's covered in it.

I reach out hesitantly, searching for that small part of her Deleriel keeps alive so he can feed on her misery, but there's nothing. Not even a small kernel of her soul left. It died, and what remains is a broken beast who is eternally hungry and full of darkness.

"Mattie." Kane leans in so he can whisper. "That thing is dead. We need to go. Now."

"I don't think we can. *Listen*. Everything that was here is gone. They're afraid of her. She's been feeding off the shades and the wraiths. The question now is *how* did she get here?"

"I don't know. Nothing can enter unless we allow it."

"Can an Angel open the doorway to the Between?"

"Well, I suppose…" He breaks off and stares at the little girl. "Deleriel let it in here to feed, didn't he?"

"My guess is he figured out what we were afraid he would. He doesn't need a doorway now. All he has to do is let them gorge on souls and then devour the child to gain all that energy."

"This is bad, Mattie. If he knows what the kids are capable of, we have a serious problem on our hands."

"You need to let your bosses know what's happening and take this soul to safety. If we're right, there may be no stopping Deleriel now."

"And what are you going to do?"

"Run. It can't chase us both, and since I have more ghost energy than you do, I'm betting it follows me."

"Mattie…"

I thrust the soul into his hands. "Go. Now!" I shove him then take off running in the opposite direction, praying for all I'm worth.

Chapter Eighteen

Snow crunches under my feet. The forest closes in around me, and all I can hear is the pounding of my heart in my ears. I refuse to look back. If I don't see her back there, it means she went after Kane, and I don't want to face that reality yet. I'm betting he can get away from her though. He just has to step back into whatever plane of existence he's going to. Me, though? I have no clue how to get back. I've opened doorways into the Between, but never one from here back to home.

It's beautiful here. A layer of white coats the barren branches of the trees.

Even as terrified as I am, the stark beauty of the place captivates me. How can something so wonderful hold things so evil, so full of hate? It boggles the mind. A loud hiss right behind me spurs my legs to run faster, but I don't think there's an escape waiting for me. I'm going to have to face the dead soul.

And I'm not sure I can fend it off. Every time one's attacked before, I've ended up unconscious and convulsing. Not the outcome I want, but the one I'll probably get.

Stop it, I tell myself. *This is not helping*. I need to stop thinking it's a foregone conclusion. I have to stay alive to help Mary, especially now that I'm pretty sure Deleriel doesn't need me to gain access to my plane of existence. I have to be strong and figure out how to deal with a dead soul.

My foot catches on a tree root buried under the snow, sending me tumbling forward. I land hard, and it knocks the wind out of me. Struggling to catch my breath, I make myself sit up and look around.

I wish I hadn't.

Not more than a foot away from me is the little girl, her eyes so hungry it makes me cringe. She's crouched, ready to spring. It reminds me of Mr. Burnett's cat when it's ready to jump at the bird it's stalked through the yard. Birds are very good at escaping. I used to giggle as I watched old Fuzzy Tail do his best to catch his prey while they teased him, just out of reach.

This little one is no Mr. Fuzzy Tail, though. It's a demonic creature whose soul has died, leaving nothing behind but the pain and rage of what happened to her in life. She's dangerous, and I'm not the birds who can fly out of reach of her clutches.

Scrambling backward, I try to get to my feet, but it's hard when you can't pull air into your lungs. The little girl pounces, pushing me back and landing on my chest, her knees on my upper arms. The feral look she's wearing is more than dangerous. It promises death.

She bares her teeth at me, hissing, and leans down. Tiny hands grip my face, and the pain is sharp and intense. And enough to bring my senses back to survival mode. I didn't survive twelve years in foster care for nothing. I don't even try to get my hands free. Using my feet, I roll over, toppling her, and then I'm up and running. Nope, not this time. I am not dying here in the Between.

More trees zing past, and the deeper I go into the white forest, the more the cold settles into my bones. It's bright, but not because of a sun shining down to warm the landscape. The Between is only a white nothingness aside from the forest. No heat source, and filled with ghosts, shades, and wraiths, it feels like it's in the negative degree range. Snow begins to fall, and I wipe it out of my eyes. Snow. Just great.

Can it even snow here? Or maybe it's my mind creating the landscape I'm seeing? The Between is exactly that, between planes. Maybe that big white landscape I saw last time I was here before Kane touched me really is what's here, and I only see trees now because that's what I think should be here?

Well, then, why did I trip over a freaking tree root?

Why am I even thinking about this right now? I toss a glance over my shoulder and slow down when I don't see the little girl following me. Where did she go? I take several deep breaths when I stop, my lungs burning from the effort of running.

I listen, straining my ears, but there's nothing. Where the heck did she go? All around me, snowflakes fall as the whisper of the wind laps at my senses. Where is the creepy little kid?

Twigs snap to my right, and I whirl in that direction. Only it's not the kid. It's a wraith. It slithers through the trees, red eyes glowing with a hunger that matches the kid. They love to find people who are half dead and suck out all their life's energy. They don't touch souls like shades do, only the life's energy of a person. I need to ask Kane how they travel from this place to ours.

Maybe Deleriel doesn't know about the ticking time bomb the dead souls are. Maybe the kids can come and go the same way wraiths do. One more question to ask later. Right now, I need to skedaddle. That wraith won't just sit there for long. Easing backward, I try to dodge around the tree, but the wraith moves with me. How am I going to get away from it?

A screeching wail rips through the veil of eerie silence. Both the wraith and I turn to see the little girl hurtling at us, her hands out and her eyes burning with rage and hunger. The wraith wastes no times and tries to run, but the little girl jumps and lands on its back. Her hands wrap around the wraith's neck, and the creature goes down.

I've never seen them feed before. Agonizing moans escape from the wraith while the little girl bends down, her stringy hair hanging like a cloak around them. Energy, a clear blue smoke, wafts up from the wraith and is inhaled by the little girl. She makes this weird sucking noise. If all you heard was the feeding, you'd think she'd latched onto some part of the creature and sucked at it much like a babe does with its mother.

There's nothing I can do for the creature. Besides, it was going to eat me. Giving them one last look, I make a run for it while she's busy. No sense in making this easy for the little undead munchkin.

My thighs begin to burn a little while later, but I press on. There is no end to this place. It's one big, long stretch of wilderness. At least all the monsters that usually lurk are hiding. One less thing to worry about, although the child is enough on her own to make up for it. When monsters hide, then you betcha it's serious.

Another ten minutes, and I have to stop and rest for a minute. I haven't run this much since middle school. Our old gym teacher used to make us run laps and would cackle when one of us dropped from exhaustion, and right now, I'm about to drop from exhaustion. This is bad. How do I get myself into these situations?

Oh, wait. Silas got me into this particular situation. I am so going to tear him a new one when I get back to his freaking lair.

Okay. I think I'm good for now, but I need to figure this out. I can open the doorway here, so why shouldn't I be able to open one back to Silas? Or even Dan? No. I can't leave Benny alone with Silas. God only knows what he'll do if I don't come back. The kid's been through enough already.

To open the Between, I have to access all the pain and anger I usually keep bottled up. This place is all that and more, and to get here, you have to need to be here. So maybe the reverse is true to get somewhere else? Love and all that happy crap?

But I'm not really a happy person. I never have been. I just do what I have to in order to survive. But Silas isn't happiness, though. What is he, then? I have to take a minute and think about that one. Silas may scare the bejesus out of me, but when I think about his studio, all I feel are sadness and grief. All those souls trapped inside a painting. It makes me sad, and the reaper in me grieves for them. I even grieve for Silas, in a way.

He may not have come out and said it, but he's doing this to free his little sister's soul from Deleriel. Everything he must have gone through over the years, all with the hope of finding her soul and releasing it.

On some level, I understand him. He's doing everything in his power to save his sister, the same way I am mine. He still scares the crap out of me, but I can relate to his motives.

A section in the trees glitches, like when you're playing a video game and it spazzes out on you. It does it again, and I go closer. I can just make out the studio and Benny on his stomach drawing. Is that it? Did I open the doorway? I run forward and slam into an invisible shield between this word and the one I desperately need to get back into.

Rubbing my forehead, I concentrate on the faint image and redouble my efforts, thinking of every sad moment in my life, and when that fails, I think about Mom and the day she died. Her smile, the crazy in her eyes, but also the love and her need to protect. I watch the light in them die until there's nothing left of my mama but an empty corpse staring at me from empty, soulless eyes. I was scared, but more than that, I hurt. She left me all alone. And from that day on, everyone left me eventually, until I was always alone. Alone and needing my mom more than anything in the world. She was everything to me, even when she was high as a kite, and I took care of her more than she did me, but she was still my mama. And I loved her.

The doorway solidifies until I can make out the dust floating in the air. I have no doubt I can get back now. Wiping the tears out of my eyes, I take a step forward, but stumble when tiny fingers clutch my ankle and drag me back. Falling flat on my face, I wrench my body around so I can see. The little girl. She must have snuck up on me when I was caught up in my memories.

I kick out with my free foot, catching her in the face, and she loosens her grip enough for me to get up and try to run, but like she did with the wraith, she jumps on my back, and her little fingers dig into the flesh around my neck.

Instant pain lashes every nerve in my body, and I fall, trying to twist so I land on top of the little urchin. Her fingers dig into my skin and hold on when we land. She's like an attack dog latched onto a burglar's arm. I can't shake her. Sitting up, I fall back and slam her into the ground as hard as I can. She doesn't make a sound, except for that creepy sucking. I know she's feeding. I can feel the flow of energy between us, but I don't know how to stop it.

Silas said I had dominion over the dead, not just ghosts. Maybe I can make her stop if I can get into her head. She's not letting go, so I reach up and place my hands on hers where they're tucked into my neck. Closing my eyes, I stop trying to fight her and let my mind get lost in her instead. I find my reaping ability, but it's hushed. Quiet. No use against this thing.

So I find that glowing light inside I used on Zeke this morning. It's hard to reach, especially when my vision blurs. This thing is sucking my energy faster

The Ghost Files – Volume 5

than I can a slush from Sonic. This is my last Hail Mary pass. Closing my eyes, I concentrate on the light and push it backward, into the little girl. It reaches out, but doesn't recoil from what it sees. I do, though. She was taken from her home by a strange man. He smelled bad and enjoyed her pain. Then she became Deleriel's snack. I can see her soul reaching out...to me.

She escaped Deleriel and came looking for me, but was pushed out. Dan...Dan and Zeke were there. I passed out, and they scared her away. This must be the little girl who first attacked me, only she wasn't trying to attack. She wanted help and I couldn't give it to her. The reaper in me demands action, but there is nothing left to be done. Her soul died, and it can't be saved.

But I have to save myself from her. Looking deeper, I can see everything. I see all the souls she's consumed, some good, some bad. I can count every molecule in her body, hold them in my hands and squeeze.

There's a popping noise that zigzags

around in my mind, like those squishy plastic packing popper thingies. There's a pause in the suckling, and I know I hurt her. She was made and can be unmade. I focus on all the atoms and molecules in her tiny body and start popping for all I'm worth. A small keening noise escapes her, and her fingers fall away from my neck, and I scramble up, keeping my mind focused on dissolving what is dead and should stay dead.

Her body is a twisting, convulsing mess with her face contorted in pain. All the souls within her cry out, afraid they'll be destroyed as well. No, they won't. I uncurl my reaper's light from where it's hiding and reach inside the girl, coaxing the souls to come to me and absorb them all, the good and the bad. Turning my attention back to the poor creature who has known only pain for so long, I find the heart of her and crush it. I watch as her body begins to dissolve into black ash that floats away gently into the falling snow.

Tears tease the edges of my vision. I didn't want to hurt her, not after realizing who she was. I was supposed to help her, but I couldn't. I failed her.

"You did not fail her, my child."

Startled, I turn to see a woman standing a few feet away from me. She's wearing a sundress, which is odd, considering we're in a freezing, snowy forest. Her golden blonde hair is done in a myriad of braids. The golden hue of her hair matches the gold in her eyes. I am so done dealing with creatures today. She's probably a lost soul that I can only screw up helping. Or she's something evil disguised in sheep's clothing. Either way, I'm out.

It only takes a moment to open the door back to Silas's studio. Once I learn how to do something, it doesn't take me long to master it. The grief I'm feeling at the loss of the little girl, combined with thoughts of my mama, are more than enough to open the doorway.

"Please, don't go."

The pain in her voice stops me, and I pause. What does she want?

"You did well. Not many can feel the pain of the gift they've been given, but you did."

"She came to me for help, and I had to kill her. I should have been able to help her."

"I have come to learn there are certain events that cannot be changed, no matter how much we wish it otherwise."

"If I hadn't passed out when she first came to me, maybe I could have helped her before her soul died." Why am I standing here talking to this woman? I don't know, but I take a few steps closer to her. I wish I knew why it's so hard to turn and walk away.

"You're very much a human." She smiles, and it's like the sun burst open in the sky above. Who is she? I take a few hesitant steps closer to her.

"Who are you, and how did you get here?"

"I heard you praying for help."

Oh. Well, I have been praying since Kane and I first saw the little girl. "Are you an Angel or something?"

"Or something." Her smile grows brighter, and the air around us warms, and some of the cold dissipates. "The soul didn't suffer long, my Rose. You did very well."

My Rose? What?

Okay, who the heck is this woman, and why is she getting all up in my business?

"I need to go…"

"I heard you crying out for help. It woke me up when nothing else could have. It's easier to hear you here, in the place between the worlds."

"*Okaaayyyy.*" I step back, toward the doorway. She's creeping me out.

"I have frightened you." Her smile falters.

Well, yeah, she's creepy, and I don't like this instinct I have to go to her. It's unnerving.

"I have to get back."

"I only just found you." She reaches out a hand. "Please don't go, not yet. Please."

"Who are you?"

"I'm your mother."

Chapter Nineteen

My mother?

She's flippin' crazy.

Stumbling backward, my only thought is to get back to Silas.

"You don't believe me." She strides forward, grasping my hands before I have a chance to escape through the doorway. "I loved you the moment I felt you growing inside me, and it nearly destroyed me to leave you, my Rose. Please, believe me. I *am* your mother."

I shake my head. Nope, nope, nope.

She tips my head up with one finger and cups my cheek, her thumb rubbing across it gently. "I used to watch you sleep for hours. You would always roll over on your stomach, and your butt would go up in the air. It amused your father very much. No matter how many times we would straighten you out, you always managed to end up in the same position. Stubborn, just like Ezekiel."

She knows Zeke's name.

"I know this must be very hard for you. You've lived all your life with your parents. Hearing me claim to be your mother is confusing."

I let out a sharp laugh. She has no idea about what kind of life I've had. "Lady, you don't know jack about me."

She frowns and her eyes go a little unfocused. What's she doing? Dan's eyes do that when he…no!

I try to pull away from her, but she catches my arm and holds me still while she goes dumpster diving in my memories. It only takes her a few seconds, but the anger that radiates off her scares me in ways even Silas can't.

"He swore to me you'd be safe."

The venom in her words spurs me to try to wrench my arm away from her, but she refuses to let me go.

"You're hurting me!" I tug at my arm again, and she lets me go, but the fury doesn't leave her.

"When I get my hands on that demon…"

"Silas?"

"Yes." Her lips curl in a snarl. "He promised you would be safe and happy."

"Silas protected me as best he could." Strange that I'm defending the demon, but it's the truth. He did protect me in his own way, and I understand now why he did what he did.

"What I saw was not protecting you." Her eyes glow a deep, deep gold, and I shiver at the menace in them.

"He got me away from Georgina, who was going to sacrifice me to a Fallen Angel to save herself, so yeah, he protected me. He healed my hands and gave me back my ability to draw. He may only have done that for his own purposes, but it meant something to me. He protected me from ghosts overwhelming my senses to the point it almost killed me. And now he's gone and given me some kind of tattoo that keeps those yellow-eyed kids from giving me seizures."

That, I'd only realized just now. That little girl should have knocked me unconscious and put my brain into full seizure mode. Those kids touching me is what originally caused the seizures. My body couldn't handle all my gifts waking up at once, and it was killing me. This time? Not even a headache when she latched on. I'm betting the headache before was a stress headache. Silas really did protect me.

Whether for himself or for me, it doesn't really matter. He kept me safe.

"But he let you suffer in those places." Bewildered, she frowns down at me.

"He didn't know." Or at least he told me he didn't know until he came looking a few years ago.

"You were supposed to be safe and happy. He promised me that."

"Look, I don't know what you thought or didn't think, but I'm okay. Being in foster care, it made me stronger than I would have been being raised in some fancy home, never having to work for anything. I learned to protect myself in foster care. I'm good. Really."

"You grew up without a mother."

I shrug. "I had a mother. She was great. I loved her."

"She tried to murder you."

"To protect me. She thought if I was dead, no one could come after me."

"That woman was not your mother." The vehemence in her voice is sharp and palpable. "You do not harm your child for any reason."

"Lady, you don't know anything about my mama, so watch yourself." The surest way to get on my bad side is to start trash talking my mother. Claire Hathaway did the best she could by me. No one will ever tell me differently. I used to blame her for everything bad that happened to me, not because it was her fault, but because I was so angry with her. Over the last year, I came to realize what a mother's love really is. Blood means jack. It's the time, the effort, the love, and the commitment that makes a parent. Not DNA.

"I may not know anything about the woman you called mother, but I do know something about being your mother. I cared for you for almost two years. I loved you."

"And you left me."

She flinches.

"I've had three mothers in my life. The first one arranged for my birth so she could give my soul to a Fallen Angel to save herself. The second agreed to bring me into the world and then abandon me. The third took on the role of my mother and never left me. She kept me through everything, even her addiction. Even when she was so high she didn't know who she was, she knew I was her kid. Yeah, she did try to kill me, but only to protect me, and then she killed herself. The junkie was my mother because she chose me over herself. She fought for me, which is something you never did. Don't stand here and try to claim to be my parent. You're not. You walked away from me voluntarily. Claire would have fought tooth and nail to keep me, no matter what bargain she might have made."

I'm panting, my chest heaving by the time I get it all out. I never realized how much rage I had pent up inside over all this. It's a relief to spew it out and cleanse my soul. Claire did leave me alone, but not voluntarily. She thought I was dead, and she was going to join me.

"The only thing I want from you is to leave Silas alone."

"As you wish, my Rose." She wears her sadness around her like a halo. "I will be here for you when you need me. All you have to do is call for me. Call my name and I will appear. Just say the word Rhea."

Not going to happen. I take three hasty steps backward, but she stops me from jumping. "One more thing. Remember Angels are made, just like every other creature in existence. Remember that, and you will not fail."

Not sure what she means, but I don't really care. I just need to get back to Benny. Falling through the doorway, I land on my butt on the hardwood floor of Silas's studio. Better than face-planting I guess, but not by much.

"Mattie!" Benny rushes over and hugs me, his little face relieved. "I was worried you wouldn't come back."

"Not a chance, kiddo. I'm Mattie Louise Hathaway, and I'm awesome."

Silas cocks an eyebrow at my statement. I shrug. I needed to confirm to myself I am who I am, I guess. I don't need that woman. I had a mother who protected me until her dying breath.

"Where is your reaper friend?" Silas wanders over to give me a hand up.

"We ran into one of Deleriel's yellow-eyed kids. I gave him Jemma's soul and told him to get it to safety, and I ran in the opposite direction."

"Are you insane?" he roars so loudly I cover my ears. "The reaper could have gotten you to safety, but you *ran*. No soul is worth your life, you little fool!"

"Stop shouting!" I yell right back. "I figured there was no point in all of us dying, so I ran. I knew it would chase me. I have more ghost energy than Kane does."

He mutters something I can't quite

catch and turns around. I get the distinct feeling he might be counting to ten to calm down. When he finally turns around, there is a fear in his eyes that wasn't there a few minutes ago. "How did you get away?"

"I killed it." The words escape in a rush. I still can't believe I did that, but it was either it or me. I survived, like I always do.

"You...killed...it."

The expression on Silas's face is priceless. It's a mix between fear, awe, and disbelief.

"Yup."

"How?" He stalks closer. "How did you kill it?"

"The how doesn't matter as much why it was there to begin with. It was a dead soul, Silas. Let loose in the Between."

He looks like I just sucker punched him. Yup, exactly what I felt like when I realized what it might mean.

"He knows."

"I think so. Not sure how, but I'm guessing he ran into one of the two running rampant through Charlotte. The one that attacked me in the Between is the first little girl who came to me at Zeke's."

"The night your seizures started."

"He doesn't need me anymore, Silas. He has all the power he could ever need."

"True, he doesn't need you, but that doesn't mean he doesn't *want* your powers." Silas smooths out the wrinkles in his shirt. His nervous habit. "Deleriel covets power. He always has, and your gifts are unique and very powerful. He'll want it even if he doesn't need it."

"I don't know, Silas."

"Trust me, Emma Rose. I know him. He's greedy."

I hope he's right. This gift is the only bargaining chip I have left to free Mary.

"Ready for your next lesson?"

My head snaps up. Another lesson?

He chuckles at my outrage. "You don't think doing it once will teach you everything you need to know, do you? Practice makes perfect, my darling girl. You know this."

And I do know it, but I hope he doesn't keep me here for weeks making me trap

souls for him.
But I'm betting he's going to.

Chapter Twenty

Three months.

That's how long Silas has kept me and Benny here in his 'home,' for lack of a better word. I've trapped hundreds of souls, and it's weighing heavily on me. Benny at least has his hound to keep him company. It's even growled at Silas a few times when he got angry with me and went anywhere near the kid. He mutters about traitorous dogs when that happens. Benny giggles, thinking it's funny. The kid misses home, but at least he seems okay. Most days, I leave him in our room when I'm doing my lessons. I know the Hell Hound will keep him safe, and I'd rather not let him see that.

I'm restless. We need to go home. I can trap a soul without even thinking about it now. Silas keeps telling me I'm not ready, but I am. I have come to think he's postponing the inevitable because he's afraid for me. It's in his eyes when he thinks I'm not looking. He always tells me I'm in his favorite, and it's a truth I've accepted over the last few weeks. I have no doubt he'd hurt me. He's done it before, but it's not something he wants to do. His first instinct is to protect me.

Weird. For a demon who could kill me as soon as look at me, he's gone out of his way to protect and prepare me for the confrontation to come. He cares in his own twisted way, I guess.

What about my life isn't weird or twisted, though?

"There you are." I look up from the kitchen table to see Silas striding into the room. "I've been looking for you. I collected a fresh batch to choose from."

"No."

His eyes squint. "No?"

"No." I put the fork down. "I am done

with this, Silas. I can do it with my eyes closed. It's time for me and Benny to go home."

"We've had this discussion before…"

"And I'm done discussing it, Silas. I will not trap another soul for you. Go ahead and strip the skin from me all you want. I'm not doing it anymore. It's time to go home."

"No, Emma Rose. I won't lay a finger on you, but I will the boy."

"And you'll get ripped to shreds. That hound of his will protect him."

"He's my hound. He'll stand down."

I laugh. "No, Silas, that dog's loyalty is to Benny. You'll never get within a foot of him, and you know it."

He mutters something unintelligible. "Do you even understand what you're saying, Mattie? If you go back, the countdown starts again, and then you'll be facing Deleriel."

"I know, but this constant waiting is doing me more harm than good. You've done well, Silas. You taught me how to do what needs to be done. I can do this. I *will* do this for Mary."

He purses his lip, and though he looks like he wants to argue, he nods. "If you're sure?"

"I am."

"Then go collect the boy, and I'll open the doorway for you."

"Can you teach me to open it?"

"Why?" Suspicion flavors his words.

"I'd like to come visit if I survive this." Weirdly, I do want to visit him. He's not as bad as I thought he was. He's lonely too. That's what I've learned, being here all these months. He's lonely, and it's something I understand well.

"You would be willing to come back here? Voluntarily?" I can't fault the disbelief he's giving me. I wouldn't have thought I'd come back either.

"Yes."

"Why?" He cocks his head, his black eyes narrowed.

"Why not?" I shrug. "You're my family, Silas. It's as simple as that."

And maybe it is that simple. I don't know.

"Okay." Silas draws the word out, like he's testing the sound or something.

There's no mistaking the spark of happiness in his onyx eyes, though. "Go collect the boy and his hound."

"You're letting him keep your hound?"

"You were right about one thing. The hound has switched loyalties. He'd grieve himself to death if I separated the two of them. Now go fetch them before I change my mind about letting you leave."

I race out of the kitchen and take several turns until I find the hallway leading to the bedroom I share with Benny. Even with Damien underfoot, the kid refuses to sleep anywhere but with me. Not that I mind. I don't like being here either. I'm used to it now, but it still freaks me out.

Benny's laid out on the bed with the Game Boy Silas brought him. I can hear the sound of Mario Kart as soon as I get close to the bed. His face is intent as he works the controls. Damien looks up and whines a welcome at me. He looks deceptively like any old dog lounging beside his owner, but I know better. He'd grow to a monstrous size, and those razor-sharp claws would rip through anything in his path. I have a healthy respect for Hell Hounds since watching them work over the last three months. I never want to be the target they've been set upon.

"Hey, kiddo, whatcha doin'?"

"Playing my Game Boy." His frown intensifies, and he leans forward, his fingers moving at lightning speed over the buttons on the small game system. "This last level is the hardest to beat."

"Well, I guess you're too busy to go home, then."

The reaction is instant. The Game Boy falls from his hands, and he leaps off the bed. "Home? Really?"

"Yup. Silas said we can go, and you can take your hound with you!"

His eyes get so big, they look like they are gonna pop out of the sockets. "I can take Damien with me? He said I could?"

"Yes." I laugh and ruffle his hair. "Now, get your things together before he changes his mind."

Benny grabs the TMNT backpack that mysteriously showed up one morning full of clothes, the Game Boy, and more games than the kid could play in a year. Silas made sure he had every creature comfort imaginable, except for a laptop or tablet. There was even a TV down here, though I'm not sure how we managed to get Direct TV in one of the inner circles of Hell.

I leave all the art supplies where I put them. I am going to come back. I meant that. Silas has taught me a lot about who I am as an artist. He pushes me, and I'm so much better than I was. Aside from the soul trapping. I'm still not sure how I grew so fond of a demon who I know will hurt me if it suits his needs. Weird. It's the term of the day.

Once Benny's collected his things, he runs from the room, his dog bounding along behind him. Not sure how well the Malones are going to appreciate their son bringing home a Hell Hound. Especially one they can't see.

"Thank you!" I hear when I round the corner and enter the studio. Benny has thrown himself at Silas in a bear hug. The demon has an uncharacteristic look of joy on his face. He hugs the kid back then pushes him away, busying himself with arranging art supplies.

"We're ready, Silas."

"Where's your bag?" He frowns.

"I don't need it. I figured I need the stuff for when I visit."

"You meant that?"

"Of course, I did." I walk into the room. "You scare the crap out of me, Silas, but you're family. Demon or not. You're my family. You stuck around, and that means something to me. Maybe only because you wanted what you engineered me for, but I'll take what I can get."

"You're talking like you're not going to make it past tonight."

"She will," Benny pipes in, petting his hound. "She's Mattie Hathaway, and she's awesome."

I laugh outright at his statement, but Silas looks worried. I can't blame him. I'm worried too. If this doesn't work, I'm dead. Can't get around that little fact.

"You still owe me a favor."

"I know. Our word is our bond. Isn't that what you're always telling me?"

"It is. Now, before you leave, I need to

transfer ownership of Damien to the boy."

"Transfer ownership?" I cock my head curiously.

"Yes. Damien technically belongs to me, and in order for him to fully obey young Benjamin, he needs to know he's his owner." Silas strides over to Benny and takes his hand, quickly slicing a deep gouge into his palm.

"Oww!" Benny yelps, but he stills when Silas forces his hand under the dog's nose. I scrunch my nose when Damien licks all the blood away. Silas says some sort of incantation, but I have no clue what it means.

"There. He's all yours now. You'll need to feed him raw, bloody meat at least once a day to keep him from eating the neighborhood pets. Do you understand?"

"Yes, sir." He nods solemnly in a way only a kid can.

"Good boy." He turns to me. "Are you ready to learn how to open the doorway into my home?"

"Yup." At least next time he kidnaps

me, I can escape and not get stuck here for another three months.

"Do not share this knowledge with anyone else, Emma Rose. If your father finds his way here, you and I will have a problem."

"I promise, I will tell no one, and Benny can't open doorways, so your secret is safe."

He hesitates a moment more, but then seems to shake off whatever concern he has and walks over to the empty wall. "Imagine a door to wherever you wish to go. In your case, your father's kitchen. Remember everything exactly as it was when you left. Remember where they were all standing. It will ground you in the space and time you were pulled from. Close your eyes and think of that moment. Do you the have the image in your head?"

"Yes."

"Open your eyes for me." He hands me a small dagger and pushes me toward the wall. "Draw a doorway on the brick with your blood. It will open up to the image you have locked into your mind."

I do as he says, thinking of everyone. Mrs. Banks doing dishes while we were talking. Caleb lounging, pretending to not be as scared about his brother as he really is for Eli's sake. Zeke and Dan sitting with me. I miss them so much. The sting of the blade is nothing compared to the thoughts of going home. I draw the outline of a door and concentrate so hard on the image in my mind, I might give myself a seizure.

At first, nothing happens, but then the wall shifts and shimmers, dissolving into an empty black nothingness. Why isn't it working?

Intent.

Dan's words echo back at me. He'd described magic as intent, and I need to intend to make this door open into that same second Silas took me. The minute my brain figures it out, the kitchen appears with my boys all panicking. Yup. That's the moment I need.

Holding out my hand to Benny, I look at Silas. "And if I want to come back?"

"Same rules apply. All you have to do is open the door back to here. I will work your blood into my wards. You'll always be able to come here. For any reason."

He's offering me a safe haven, but is it because he thinks I'll fail, and Deleriel will kill me? Hard to say.

"I'll see you soon." Benny and I step through the doorway and into my dad's kitchen.

They all turn and stare at me, open-mouthed, but then Benny launches himself at Eli, who gathers the kid close, all the while staring at me like I'm some kind of wonder. Much better than his death stare.

"Hello, boys."

Chapter Twenty-One

Dan beats my dad to me and wraps me in a bear hug tighter than usual. He stinks of fear. Yes. During my three-month foray into the inner circles of Hell, it's another trick I picked up. I can smell emotions.

"Can't breathe!" I manage to twist my face enough to drag in puffs of air. The boy is seriously terrified, but among all that, I smell what I associate love with—honey. It's a feeling of home and family unlike anything I've ever known. And it's all uniquely Dan.

"I swear, if you do not hand me my daughter…" Zeke's angry growl isn't even enough for Dan to let me go.

"What happened?" He buries his nose in my hair. "How did you get away?"

"We didn't." Benny lets go of Eli and hurls himself at Dan, who is forced to let me go so he can catch the kid. Zeke wastes no time in pulling me into a hug.

"What do you mean, you didn't?" Dan picks the little boy up like he weighs nothing and wraps him in just as big of a bear hug before handing him to Caleb. I've never seen Caleb cry before, not even when Dan was in the hospital, but he has tears streaming unabashedly down his cheeks when he holds his baby brother close.

"Silas let us come home. And he gave me a dog!"

Zeke goes stock still, understanding immediately what the kid meant. "A dog?" His eyes sweep the kitchen, but he can't see Damien. Benny and I can. Silas told me that we'll be able to see any Hell Hound now because we've been given the ability to do so with magic.

"Yeah. His name's Damien. He's awesome."

"Damien?" Eli cracks a smile. "You named your dog Damien?" I know what he's thinking. That old movie, *The Omen*. Freaks his mom out.

"No. It was his name already." He squirms, and Caleb lets him down. The kid snaps his fingers, and the men watch, fascinated, as the air seems to move with the hound who comes to sit at Benny's side.

"Um, Benny, I don't think Mom will let you keep a Hell Hound."

"'Course she will. He's a good hound. Aren't you, boy?" He scratches the dog behind the ears, and it leans into him. That beast loves him.

"What did Benny mean, you didn't escape?" Zeke hugs me tighter. "That Silas let you go?"

"Remember I told you Silas wouldn't let me die before he got what he wanted from me?" At Dan's nod, I continue. "He said what Dan wanted to do would work, and I might even have been able to make the sketch he wanted, but it would turn my brain to mush in the process."

"What?" Dan stares at me, horrified.

"Like I said, Silas wasn't about to let me do something that would ruin his chances of getting what he wanted. So he took me and gave me some kind of ancient spelled tattoo to protect me. It worked too. When one of Deleriel's little yellow-eyes creatures attacked me, I never felt a thing and was able to hold onto the memories."

"Where were you?" Zeke absently rubs my back, I think more to soothe himself than me. He still hasn't let go.

"In Silas's home, one of the inner circles of Hell."

His hiss is chock-full of rage. "I will kill him."

"No, you won't. If it weren't for Silas, I'd be dead right now. And it's because of Silas I know how to deal with Deleriel. I sat there for three months and practiced."

"Three months?" Dan's confusion is palpable. "You were only gone for a few minutes."

"Time moves differently there," Zeke tells him. "A second here is however long it needs to be in Hell. It could be minutes, hours, days, months, or years."

"Before we get too deep into this, Eli, call your mother and let her know Benny's here. I need to go help Dan with his drawing while we wait for them to get here."

"How do you have Benny?" Eli inches closer, his eyes fathomless.

"I made a deal with Silas, remember?" I smile sadly. "I gave him anything he wanted if he'd get him. And he did. He said he fished him out of the trunk with just a few bruises. Nothing bad happened to him."

"I was scared in the trunk, but the man told me he came to rescue me. He had black eyes, Eli, and I knew that meant a demon. He took me, and the next thing I knew, I found Mattie asleep in one of the rooms. She protected me."

"The demon tried to hurt you?" Eli's voice is so soft, I can barely hear it. He's mad.

"No. He was nice to me. Got me a Game Boy too." He points to the backpack strapped to his shoulders. "We watched cartoons, ate pizza, and played video games."

"Nice to you?" Eli frowns. "Benny, what did you promise him in return?"

"Nothing." The kid shrugs. "He was just nice to me."

"That makes no sense."

"Silas never makes sense." Best to get things moving. I don't have a lot of time before tonight. "Call your mom, Eli. She's going out of her mind with worry right now."

"You made a deal for my brother." Eli steps closer. "Thank you."

"No big deal."

"It is a big deal." Zeke leans back until he can look me in the eyes. "What did you promise him, Emma Rose?"

"A favor. Nothing more, nothing less."

"Not your soul?"

"Nope. He said I would have no bargaining chip with Deleriel if the Angel sensed my soul already belonged to another demon. Now, Zeke, let me go so I can grab my sketchbook and help Dan out with his sketch."

"But you just said Silas took you because…."

"But he also inked me with some kind of super tattoo that will protect my human body from all the supernatural elements that can kill it. It'll be fine, Papa, I swear."

Turning, I run out of the kitchen and up the stairs to Dan's room, where I left my sketch book. It's only as I'm holding my pad I realize I called Zeke Papa. The knowledge staggers me for a moment, and I sink down in the chair. I called him Papa. I'm not sure what to think about that. Did it even register with Zeke I'd done it? I bet it had, and he thinks I'll be saying that all the time now. Should I? I mean, I might not live through the night. Why not make him happy?

I guess three months of missing him made me rethink the whole keeping him at arms-length thing I was unconsciously doing. He's my father. I saw what I meant to him and what he'd do to protect me. He's earned the title.

Shaking my head, I grab my charcoal pencil off the nightstand. I guess I'll play it by ear with the Papa thing. If Zeke doesn't make a big deal out of it, then neither will I.

The cold slams into me with the force of a baseball driven by a one hundred mile per hour pitch. Right in the back of the head, and I go down, my things falling from my hands as I blink back the instant blurriness.

Gritting my teeth, I push up off the floor and look around. Nothing.

"Who's in here?" I demand, getting to my feet. "I'm warning you now, I don't have any issues opening a doorway to the Between and tossing you in to be food for the boogeymen that live there."

A low chuckle resounds through the room. It's not a very nice sound either. Maybe whatever's in here isn't afraid of the Between.

The sound of the sink being turned on in the bathroom sends chills up my back. What is it with ghosts and bathrooms? Do they have an unspoken rule that you have to scare people in the bathroom? I bet the little buggers do.

I sprint for the door and find it locked. I can't get it open. Another of those spine-chilling laughs echoes around me. I see the ice starting to creep from under the bathroom door, spiraling out like a spider's web.

"What do you want?" I scan the room, wiling the thing to show itself.

"You." The cool breath ghosts across my ear, and I jump, nearly falling. The temperature takes a nosedive, and I can see my breath coming out in little puffs of steam.

"Well, you can't have me."

"So much light..." Fingers trail along my arm, and I leap away from the door, diving toward the other side of the room. The malice in the ghost's touch is enough to send waves of fear through me. This thing means to do me serious harm. Without even thinking about it, I open a doorway to the Between in a circle around me. If that thing wants me, it's going to have to cross the barrier and potentially get sucked into the void.

Using the Between as a weapon is not a good thing. Living reapers who did it in the past became the shades that live there, but dang it, I am done being a victim. I've been there, done that, and won't do it again. Ice creeps along the walls, covering the furniture and the windows in what feels like seconds. It so cold, my nose is burning.

"You've been feeding, little reaper."

Where is it? Why can't I see the ghost? It's the one thing I hate about this ability. I can't force them to show themselves. It's aggravating and terrifying at the best of times.

The cold intensifies, and the sweat beads on my skin start to ice over. This ghost is old, powerful. Probably something like Jonah. He was the ghost I faced in New Orleans. He'd been feeding off the souls he'd had trapped in the house until he was almost unstoppable. If not for Eric's sacrifice of his own soul, I wouldn't have been able to stop him. That is not an option now.

"Who are you? Show yourself!"

That low chuckle rumbles around the room.

"I'm not afraid of you."

"Yes, you are." The words slither through my skull, and I flinch at the pinpricks of pain they cause.

264

Well, I might be a little afraid, but not enough to let him in my head and twist it. "Think so, buster? Come closer and show yourself, then you'll see how afraid of you I really am."

"Brave." Another laugh rattles through the room. "Foolish, but brave."

The cold edges closer, and I hear the first wails of the shades circling the opening I'd made into their world. They're as hungry as the ghost taunting me. I will throw him in. No hesitation. If that makes me a bad person, so be it.

"Mattie!"

The pounding on the door only makes the ghost laugh harder. "They cannot save you from me." And with that, I'm hit again and thrown backward, my back hitting the wall, and I slide down it, stunned.

Hands grip me, cold hands that burn.

"Open the door, Hilda!" More pounding, but I can't focus on that, only on the sensation of energy leaving me. It's like a small cut and someone pinching and pushing on the skin, forcing blood to the surface. Feeding from the souls I reaped. A crushing sense of failure grips me, and I struggle to see any hope. It sucks all the joy and happiness from me.

"No!"

I haven't survived all this to go out like a wuss. I harness that which makes me a reaper and lash out, wrapping the bands of blue light around the air in front of me. A shape takes form as it struggles to free itself. A man, late thirties, an ugly hole in his right shoulder. It looks like someone or something tore a hole clean through. He's pulsing with energy, souls he's devoured.

Kane, I whisper furiously, needing help. *Kane, get your butt down here now*!

He pops in right beside me and gasps. "What are you doing wrestling with a wraith?"

"Trying not to get eaten!" I double my efforts to hold it still. "Can I throw it in the Between without blackening my soul?"

"Well, duh. It's a wraith. That's where they're supposed to be."

"Can you reap the souls it's eaten?"

"Why don't you?"

"Kinda busy here keeping it from, you know, eating me!"

The door bursts inward, and Dan, Eli, Caleb, and Zeke all stumble in, stopping to stare at me.

"What is that thing?" Dan rushes over, but I warn him off. If he gets too close, it might try to lash out at him. Any more energy, and it'll be too strong for me to hold.

"It's a wraith." Zeke comes closer, but stops shy of just where Dan is. "The question is, how did it get in the house?"

"You took down the ghost-proofing!" I grit my teeth against the pain jackknifing through my skull as the wraith attempts to make me turn it loose. "Kane, you'd best get reaping, or these souls are lost."

"Kane?" Zeke looks around. "Who's Kane, and where is he?"

Dan's face pales as it does every time he hears the reaper's name who came for him. He always has this fear in the back of his mind the reaper will change his mind and take him. It's not one he's ever voiced, but I know him well enough to know it's there.

"A reaper." Dan inches backward, confirming my suspicions.

"Why can't I see him?" Zeke looks a little put out. He is a living reaper, after all. It stands to reason he should be able to see him.

"He doesn't want you to." I lock my elbows. "Do it now, Kane, or they are going into the Between with him."

Kane mutters something about not rushing him, and I want to slap him. He's not the one holding a beast who wants to eat him whole. "Hurry up!"

"Hold him still. This is going to hurt."

And he isn't joking. As soon as Kane starts harvesting souls, the wraith lets out this eerie howl that makes everyone in the room jump. Even Damien wanders in and growls so low, it's even more menacing than usual. He stalks over to me and sniffs. Another hair-raising sound emanates from the hound, but I don't even know how to describe it except to say any other time, I'd run and not look back, praying for all I'm worth not to let whatever was behind me catch me.

Benny has a Hell Hound. You tend to forget what that really means when you're around a tame one. But he's not tame. He's a freaking Hell Hound! It's something we should never forget.

"Good boy," I whisper. "Please don't eat me."

"He's not going to eat you." Benny shoves in between his brothers. "What are you doing on the floor?"

"You can't see the thing I'm trying to keep still?"

He shakes his head. "Damien can, I think. It's why he wouldn't stop until I let him out. He doesn't like it."

"It's a wraith." A cry is ripped from me when another band of pain hits right behind the eyes. "Kane, hurry up. This hurts."

"One more minute…done. Throw it back."

He doesn't have to tell me twice. I pick the thing up, and using the light holding it, I drag it down into the Between, letting loose and closing the opening in one breath. He reaches down a hand to me and pulls me up.

"Thanks." I lean over, taking deep breaths and trying to dissipate the pain ratcheting around in my head. Silas said it wouldn't kill me, not that it wouldn't hurt.

"You're glowing again." Kane comes closer and sniffs me. "What happened when you ran from me in the Between?"

Silas blocked Kane from coming back when he discovered that the reaper actually listened to me and took the soul to safety. He said no one was allowed near me who didn't put my safety first, including my would-be tutor in the art of reaping.

"I reaped the souls the kid swallowed." I put up a hand to ward off his outrage. "I wasn't about to let them die with her, so don't give me grief about it."

"Any idea what she's talking about?" Eli whispers to Caleb, who shakes his head.

"I'm going to take these souls through the Between, but I'll have an ear to the ground for you, Mattie. If you need me, just call." Kane looks worried, but he also needs to get gone before something else comes looking to see why there is such a concentrated amount of ghost energy in one place. No need to turn Zeke's into a smorgasbord for the demented, power-hungry monsters.

"Did you two call your parents?" I straighten up then sit down in the chair I'd vacated earlier. Damien comes over and licks my face. Eww. So gross. I hate when he does that. He knows I can't stand doggie slobber, and he does it on purpose.

Benny giggles when I push the hound away. "Down, Damien."

As per usual, the hound whines and lies down at my feet, one big paw over both of mine. The dog will always pick Benny over me, but he likes me too.

"Yeah, they're on their way over here." Eli inches closer, his eyes down, trying to figure out where the dog is.

"He won't hurt you."

Unless Benny tells him to, but I keep that little tidbit to myself. Besides, Benny would never hurt his brothers for any reason. I'm not worried.

"Hell Hounds are bred to hurt you," he

argues and squats a good foot from where the hound is eyeing him curiously. "It's their only purpose."

"They're bred to obey their masters," I disagree. "It's not their fault their masters are usually demons who want nothing but to maim and kill people." I lean down and scratch Damien's ears, something he loves. "He's a good hound, and Benny will make sure he stays that way."

Neither of the Malone boys looks like they believe me, but tough. Benny is not giving his hound away, not when it'll protect him with its life.

"Hilda, can I talk to you?"

The softness in Eli's tone makes me look up. His eyes are swimming in grief, remorse, and shame. Oh, so, now he feels bad about blaming me for everything, does he?

"Not alone." The cold bite in Dan's voice impresses even Zeke, I think. He stands taller and straighter, the sword blazing against his back. It makes me see the man he's going to grow into. Eli is powerful in his own right, Guardian Angel juice and all that, but he has nothing on Dan.

"No, not alone," I agree. The whole Guardian Angel thing makes me feel safe, and all my worries disappear when he touches me. He is what I need him to be. Usually, that's a furnace to keep me warm, but right now, I need a clear head. I figured a lot of stuff out while I was at Silas's. It's easy to do when you don't have them all jabbering away at you every day, pulling you in a million different directions.

Eli looks hurt, but I don't care. I can't let myself care. This needs to be done.

"Let's go out on the balcony."

Stiffening my spine, I turn and walk out of the room, leaving Dan and Eli to follow me.

Chapter Twenty-Two

I'm a little shocked Zeke didn't try to stop us from leaving, especially after Silas's drive-through snatch and grab heist. I head straight for the balcony overlooking the city. It's barely noon. The sun is blazing in a cloudless sky, the blue so brilliant it defies logic. The type of blue that inspires a painter. The type of blue I'd sit and draw for hours at a time. I do wonder if it'll be the last blue sky I get to see.

"Hilda."

"Don't call me that." Even now, months later for me, I still hate that nickname.

Turning, I see Dan closing the French doors and coming to stand beside his brother. They look so different. Dan's dark brown hair and even deeper brown eyes are a shocking contrast to Eli's blond hair and aqua eyes. They share the same mouth and nose, but that's where the similarities end. Looking at them, you'd never guess they were brothers.

"I'm sorry." He scuffs his shoes on the stone floor. "I blamed you for what happened to Benny, and it was wrong. I was scared and angry, and I took it out on you. I'm so sorry, Hilda." He takes two steps toward me, and I put up a hand to stop him.

"No, stay over there, Eli. You'll make everything I'm feeling go away if you touch me, and I need to say a few things to you."

He stops and looks at me curiously. "What do you mean?"

"You're my Guardian Angel, Eli. You are what I need you to be. Sometimes a furnace, sometimes the person who will make all my worries go away. My confidant, my cheerleader. Right now, I need for all this hurt and pain to go away, and if you touch me, that's exactly what will happen. At least until you leave, and then it'll rush back. It'll be debilitating to me if it goes away for just a bit and then comes back. I need to feel this to say what I need to say."

"I didn't know."

"I didn't understand the magnitude of it myself until I spent three months without someone to take all the hurt away, even for a little while. This bond between us, it muddled everything up. I like you, Eli. A lot. But is it the bond strengthening itself any way it can? I don't know. I don't think we'll ever know."

"Is that bad, though, in the end? I think it only magnifies what we truly feel."

"Yeah, Eli, it's a bad thing. I don't want to feel this way about someone who doesn't trust me, and blames me for everything."

"Hilda…"

"Don't call me that, it's not my name." The hurt I'm feeling lashes out at him with every word. "The thing is, I know what I felt had some truth to it. Otherwise, what you did wouldn't have hurt so much. It cut me to ribbons thinking you hated me."

"I didn't hate you."

"You don't want to be my Guardian Angel, Eli."

"Yes, I do." He takes two steps in my direction, and Dan catches him by the back of his shirt and hauls him back. I flash him a grateful smile. Eli glares at Dan, but stops trying to move forward. "Really, I do."

"Maybe now you do, but when it mattered, you despised the fact the bond made you protect me. Even earlier, when you came to check on me, it wasn't because you *wanted* to do it. The bond drove you to do it, and I saw how much you hated the fact you had to. Don't try to deny it."

"I was working through it." He shoves his hands in his pockets. Such a Dan move. "I knew it was wrong to feel like that, but I couldn't help it. He was just an innocent little boy who wouldn't have been here to get taken if not for you asking Dan to help you find your dad. It brought all this in our lap."

"I sped up the timeline, yeah, I'll give you that." I lean against the rails. "But Zeke was right. Your dad would have come here. Would he have uprooted all of you and brought you with him? I don't know. Only you can answer that."

"If he was going to be gone for more than a few months, then yes, he would have." The words are torn from him. He knows he did wrong.

"Then Benny would have been in danger anyway. Knowing me had nothing to do with them taking the son of the chief investigating officer on the case. Did it?"

"No."

"Then why would you blame me?" Pain flares in my voice, and I beat it back. Three months of thinking about this made up my mind.

"I...I'm sorry." He looks miserable, but I won't let my resolve weaken. Not when it comes to protecting myself.

"You can't have had any real feelings for me outside of that 'oh, she's cute, let me ask her out' kinda thing."

"I did, Mattie. I swear it."

"No, Eli. You didn't. Wanna know how I know?" I don't give him a chance to nod or tell me no. "You left, Eli. You found out I was part demon, and you walked away. Sure, it was only to the store around the corner to talk it over with your sister, but you did leave, Eli. Everyone who's ever mattered me has walked away from me."

"Except Dan."

I nod. "Except Dan. He meant it when he said he was in it for the long haul. I've pushed him away at every turn, done my best to make it hard for him to stick around, but he did. If anyone should blame me for the bad things that have happened in their life, it's Officer Dan. I ruined everything for him and his family. Destroyed it, really. But he never blamed me, not once."

"You can't compare us, Hilda. Dan didn't understand what demons really were, what they're capable of..."

"Yes, Eli, I do." Dan lays a hand on his brother's shoulder. "I understand perfectly who and what they are. I got tied down and experimented on by Silas. He almost killed me. I know who they are, but I know Mattie too. It's what kept me there when I discovered the same demon who almost killed me was her grandfather. Doesn't matter what blood runs in her veins. She's no more evil than Benny. Look at what she did to get our little brother back. She made a deal with a demon for him. That's who Mattie Louise Hathaway is. She's strong, tough, and loyal to a fault. She went to bat for the kid, and it didn't matter what it cost her. That's who she is. She's everything that is good and kind in this world. If you can't recognize that, then you don't deserve her."

"I screwed up." Eli takes a ragged breath. "How can I make this right, Hilda?"

"You can't." I rub my temple, the headache almost blinding at this point.

"You have to let me make this right, Hilda. We haven't even gotten that first date."

"And we won't get that first date." I'm

not about to let anyone cause me to doubt myself anymore. That's what Eli does. He looks at me and is always wondering about my motives. He'll never see past the demon blood I have. I can read the simple truth in his eyes every time he looks at me. I won't do that to myself. I deserve better than that. No one should ever make me feel the way I did the night I told him about my demon blood and he left me there, crying and feeling like I was worthless.

And Dan made it better. Like he always does.

"Hilda, please."

"No, Eli. Once we get through this thing with Deleriel, we're done. I don't know how that will work, you being my Guardian Angel, but we'll figure it out. You're a part of Dan's life, so you'll always be part of mine because of that."

"But?"

"But only as my friend. Maybe one day you'll be family to me like Dan and Mary, but I have to get past all this pain first."

"So, you're choosing Dan over me?"

His beautiful aqua eyes are swimming with so much pain, it's hard not to reach out and comfort him.

"No. I'm choosing *me*." I take several deep breaths. "I had months to think about this. I spent so much time shielding myself from any kind of hurt, I didn't even know what love was. Dan helped me figure out what it means to let someone take care of me, to love me. He's the reason I am who I am today. But I don't know this girl. I'm afraid of her on my best days. I have to figure out how to be her without fear before I can let anyone else in. Including Dan."

Dan's stoic cop face is in place, but I hurt him. I know it. I'm telling truths here, and if he can't understand it, I don't know what to do or say to make him understand.

"When this is over, I'm going to New Orleans. I'm going to go and be Emma Rose Crane. No one knows me there. They don't know about my rap sheet or the poor, pathetic foster care kid who doesn't understand how to love. I can start over and figure out how Mattie

Louise Hathaway, foster kid, can fit into this new person I've become over the last year. I want to learn to mesh the two so I can be a better person. You made me want to be a better person. For me. Can you understand that, Officer Dan?"

"More than you know." He walks over and gives me his famous bear hug before letting me go. "You can do anything, Mattie Louise Hathaway. You don't need me or anyone. Go be you and not who everyone else wants you to be." He holds my head in his hands, and I struggle to keep my tears in. "Go, live your life and be happy."

Only Officer Dan would put me before his own pain. I lean up and kiss him. Really kiss him. And those fireworks I was missing before? They explode when he wraps me in his arms and kisses me back. It's like the word melts away, and everything we both want to say is in the way our lips move, the way we hold onto each other like it's life and death. He loves me enough to let me go. And I love him enough to go and become the better person he believes I am.

When he pulls away, his eyes are serious. "I love you, Mattie. When you become Emma Rose Crane, don't forget Mattie Louise."

"I won't. Promise." Laying my head on his chest, I snuggle into him, content and feeling more like I'm home than I have in my entire life. Dan is home to me. Always will be.

"I think I'll go inside." Eli turns to go, and as much as I hate causing him pain, this is for the best. He needs to move on.

"You know, even when you go to New Orleans, you're not getting rid of me." Dan lays his head on mine. "I'm going to Skype you to death."

"I wouldn't have it any other way."

"You asked me to come with you to New Orleans, but I can't, Mattie. I have to be here for Dad and Cam through Mom's trial. I can't leave them."

"I know. I knew it the second the words left me. You don't abandon your family, Dan. It's not who you are."

"I do have one request to make of you, Squirt."

"What?"

"I need you here when Mom goes to trial. I don't think I can do it by myself."

"You don't think I intended to let you suffer through that alone? I'll have my butt parked right beside you in the courtroom, no matter how many death glares your mom throws at me."

He chuckles. "I'm going to miss my daily dose of sass from you."

"I'm going to miss our breaking and entering shenanigans."

He laughs outright. "I love you."

"I love you too. Now, let's go and do a more accurate drawing of our Fallen Angel possessed pedophile and try to get him under lock and key before my big showdown with Deleriel."

His arms tighten at Deleriel's name. "You're going to be fine. You've survived everything else thrown at you. You'll survive this too."

"Of course, I will. I'm Mattie Louise Hathaway, and I'm awesome."

Chapter Twenty-Three

Eli is conspicuously absent when we go back inside. I'm not surprised. He's in pain. So am I. It hurt to let him go more than I like to admit, but I deserve someone who doesn't judge me at every turn. Caleb doesn't say anything, but he doesn't have to. He knew before I did how this would end. I've seen it in his expression every time he's in the room with me, Dan, and Eli. He just nods and turns back to whatever he was talking about with Josiah. He and Lila have managed to find their way into the kitchen.

"We need to fix this, Mama." Zeke

runs a hand through his long hair. "We cannot protect her with the ghost-proofing down."

"Yes, darling, but she can't get in with it up."

"Especially now." They all turn to me questioningly. "I reaped over three dozen souls from the yellow-eyed kid who was let loose in the Between."

Lila sucks in a shocked gasp. "No wonder that thing came here. You must be glowing like the sun to them."

"Pretty much. Can someone get my sketchpad for me? I'm not up to going and finding another wraith lurking and waiting to catch me alone."

"I'll do it." Dan lets me go and heads upstairs.

"Come with me for a few minutes, *ma petite*." Zeke takes my hand leads me to the office. "Are you okay? I saw Eli leave a few minutes ago. He looked like he might have been dashing tears away."

I sag onto his comfy sofa and pull my knees up. "I told him goodbye."

"Goodbye?"

"I like, Eli, but I like *me* more. He

makes me feel like I'm not good enough, and I deserve better than that, Papa. Maybe that's selfish, but I'm tired of trying to live up to someone else's ideals."

"Of course, you deserve better." He sits down and turns so he can face me. "Never let anyone make you feel like that, Emma Rose. Never."

"I want to go to New Orleans with you after all this is over. Try to be Emma Rose, if that's okay with you? Being Mattie hasn't brought me much of anything but chaos and pain."

"I think being Mattie has brought you a lot more than you realize, sweetheart." He tips my head up so I'm looking at him. "It brought you the ability to survive where others wouldn't. It gave you strength and determination. You found Dan and the Crosses, and even that social worker of yours. They'd all move mountains for you. Don't dismiss Mattie Hathaway out of turn."

I smile. "I thought you'd jump at the chance to call me Emma Rose permanently."

"Oh, I will." His own grin overtakes him. "You've always been Emma Rose to me, and it's hard to remember to call you anything but that. I'm just saying, don't try to erase Mattie Hathaway and become someone you're not."

"Dan literally just said the same thing to me."

"I like that boy. I didn't think I would, especially considering how he feels about my only child, but I do like him. He's honorable. You chose well."

"I didn't choose him either."

Zeke cocks and eyebrow at me.

"I chose me. I want to figure out who I am without relying on everyone else around me. I need to find a way to be Emma Rose and Mattie, and I need to do it on my own."

"You said goodbye to them both?"

"Sorta. Dan will always be a part of my life, and in the future, he will be mine, but for right now, I need to be me for me and no one else. Does that make sense?"

"Perfect sense." He pushes my hair out of my face. "You are much smarter than I was at your age."

"I doubt that." I sigh and wrap my arms around my knees. "Can Mary come with us? She needs out of here just as badly as I do. Neither of us can escape the memories of what happened to us. Our nightmares wake each other up. I can't leave her behind. I thought maybe you could pull some strings and get her into Tulane?" I know we talked about us going to New Orleans earlier, but I feel the need to reaffirm my decision to leave Charlotte and everything it holds behind me.

He frowns. "I would love to offer her a home, *ma petite*, but she may not be in any shape to…"

"You think Deleriel will break her." I've thought of this too. It's plagued my thoughts every minute of every day. She can't do confinement.

"I'm afraid she's not going to be the same person she was, that's all."

"Even so, I can't leave her. If she needs help, we'll get her help, but we'll do it in New Orleans."

"If that's what you want, and it's okay

with her mother, then that's what we'll do."

"Thank you." I debate telling him about my meeting with the being who is my mother, but I'd made up my mind before I'd been snatched to tell him everything. "I met my mother in the Between."

"Amanda? I thought you told me she crossed over."

"No, not Mama. My mother. The one who inhabited Georgina's body."

Zeke just stares, unable to form words. I know that feeling.

"I reacted badly."

"You always do when you're forced to deal with something you're not ready to deal with yet." Dan walks into the room carrying my art supplies. "It's who you are, Squirt. You hit first and ask questions later. I'm betting you screamed at her and told her to get lost because she's not your real mother."

Nail. Head.

"Well, she kept harping on and on about being my mom, and it's not true. She basically made a deal, and instead of fighting to keep me, she walked away from me. Just gave me away like I was something to be bartered. It's not right that she thinks she can simply step in and take up where she left off fifteen years ago."

"Mattie, what is Silas always saying to you about deals?" Dan hands me my stuff and sits on the other side of me.

"That our word is our bond. You can't break a deal."

He stares at me expectantly.

"It shouldn't apply to your flesh and blood."

"But it does." Zeke leans forward, his eyes aflame with acceptance of her actions. "Deals are deals. They cannot be broken in the supernatural world."

"What happens if you do?"

"Your forfeit your life."

My eyes widen. "What?"

"It's an old rule, created when the first demons were spawned. It's what kept them in check then and keeps them in check now. The law applies to any supernatural creature, though, including us."

"Before you pass judgement on her, maybe you should think about it first?" Dan gives me his crooked grin. "I'm not saying forgive and forget, just think about what she went through before you cast her aside. Will you at least try to do that?"

I nod. I can do that. Maybe.

"Enough about this. Let's try this Vulcan mind meld thingy." I'd rather deal with a massive headache than family issues.

"*Star Trek*? Really?"

"What?" I shrug, unashamed. "I love that show. Picard was awesome. Don't think you're getting out of going to a convention with me this year, either. I'm decking you out as a Romulan."

"Uh, no, thank you." He tries to hide his laughter, but it's there. He's a closet Trekkie. I know it.

"So, how does this thing work?" I flip open my sketchbook to a blank page and grip the charcoal pencil just a little nervously.

"No clue, Squirt."

"It's your gift. You should know

something!"

"Well, I'm usually touching something when I get a vision."

"The boy. You need to touch him, since he was the last one abducted." Zeke gets up and goes to the library door, shouting for Caleb to bring Benny.

Something occurs to me. "Why haven't we heard of another kid going missing since Benny isn't in their possession anymore?"

"There might have been another abduction, but we've all be so focused on Benny we missed it." Dan looks troubled. "He's had some other kid all this time, and no one's out looking for them."

"I'm sure there are people out looking. They would have been reported missing, and when it's a little kid, they don't enforce the twenty-four-hour spiel."

Benny charges into the room, Damien on his heels. The hound loves to run. I hope the Malones have a big back yard. "I'm heeeere!"

"I can see that, kiddo. You up for helping me and Dan?"

"Sure." He hops up and snuggles into

my side. "Whatcha need, Emma Rose?"

Benny has taken to calling me Emma Rose. It's all Silas used while we were with him, and the kid got used to it.

"Well, Dan has this superpower that lets him see things."

"Really?" he squeals. "That's so cool!"

"I know, right?" I ruffle his hair. "So, this might be scary."

"Can't be scarier than when I snuck the last pudding cup out of the fridge Silas said was his."

I burst out laughing. "You did that? You swore you didn't."

He shrugs. "I wasn't going to 'fess up when he was so mad."

"I think I rubbed off a little too much on you, kid." He sounds so much like me now.

"That might not be such a bad thing," Caleb surprises me by saying. "I think having a little dose of Mattie Hathaway will make him stronger."

"Couldn't hurt, I guess. Now, Benny. Dan is going to hold your hand, and then he's going to see things that are important to you. Funny things, embarrassing things, things you love, things you hate, but he's looking for one particular thing."

"What?"

"The man who took you and threw you in the trunk."

"I don't want to think about that." He buries his head under my arm. "Please don't make me."

The kid starts to shake, and if there were any other way, I'd do it, but there's not. "Benny, I need you to be brave. There's another little boy or girl who took your place in the trunk, and we need to find them. You're the only person who can help us. I know you can be brave enough to do the right thing."

"Brave like you?" He lifts his head up.

"Like me?"

He nods solemnly. "Yes, you protected me even when Silas made you do bad things. You tried to make sure I didn't see it."

What am I supposed to say to that?

"Silas would get so mad and threaten me to make you do what he wanted. He's a bad man, even when he's not. You're a good person, even when you do bad things."

Again, he leaves me speechless.

"If you want me to brave like you were, then I can be brave."

This kid. He amazes me daily.

"You're awesome, kid."

"Same as you." He grins up at me, but I can still see the fear behind the bravado. So much like me. Maybe being a little like me will keep him from getting killed when he starts hunting like his brothers.

"Okay. Dan's going to hold your hand, and I'm going to hold Dan's hand. Hopefully, I'll see what he sees. I need you to think back to the day the man took you. Remember it as best you can. It's hard, I know, and more than a little scary, but I need you try, kiddo."

"I will."

"Ready?"

He nods and gives me one hand and Dan the other while I slip my free hand into Dan's. I hope this works. Otherwise, we've just made him relive the scariest moment of his life for nothing.

Zeke comes over and sits on the coffee

table, facing all three of us. "This is unusual, to say the least. Dan, have you ever forced a vision before?"

"No, but if the memory is fresh enough, I should see it. It didn't take much when I touched the bear in the lab. I just don't know if Mattie will be able to see it or not."

"The two of you are connected, yes? Like you are with Eli?"

"Not exactly." This from Caleb. "Eli is her Guardian Angel. He will always know when she's in trouble or needs him. He can always find her, no matter where she is. That bond is hardwired into her emotions. The one she and Dan share is different. I saw it when I first met them. One of my gifts is to see auras. Her and Dan's auras were interconnected, even before they were soul-bonded. Dan has an innate need to protect her because it's in our blood to do so, but his connection is stronger than ours because she chose him to protect her. Does that transfer into her being able to see his visions? I don't know."

"Well, we won't know if it'll work

unless we get on with it." I'm done talking. Benny's hand is shaking. We need to get this done with the least amount of trauma possible. "Benny, close your eyes and think really hard about that day. Dan, do your thing and I'll…well, I don't know, but I'll try something."

Benny does what I tell him, and Dan stares at the kid. His eyes get unfocused, a sure sign he's seeing what Benny is showing him. My turn. I have Shaman blood in me. I've seen visions before. This shouldn't be hard. Right?

Wrong.

As much as I concentrate and try to force my way into Dan's head, the worse my own headache gets. This is not working. So, what would work? Instead of focusing on the vision, I focus on Dan. I let everything fall away except for Officer Dan Richards. The room melts, the people in it go away, and all I'm left with is Dan. There is a thick cord of blazing white light tethered between us. Is this what Caleb was talking about? If it is, it's beautiful.

Then I see Dan. All he was, all he is,

and all he can be. He's strength, courage, and determination. He defines what makes a good person. He always will. I see him as a little boy, clinging to his mother, arguing with Cam, and as a teenager, his head bowed as his father lectures him. Disappointing his father disturbed him deeply. He loves his family. I see him as a police cadet, trying to do what he feels is right, even though his mother begs him to do something less dangerous. Dan has a built-in need to protect, and that's what pushed him toward the police force. It's who he is.

I can feel my own aura pulse around his, and I follow the strong pull, letting it guide me to what he desperately wants me to see. I feel his iron will shoving the images at me. All I have to do is open my eyes and see them.

They slam into me with a force unlike anything I've ever known. My head explodes in pain, but I can see it.

Benny was playing in the back yard. His mother called for him to stay where she could see him from the window. He ignored her. He was digging, sure he'd found some cool relic like an arrowhead. So focused on his task, he failed to hear the gate squeak open, or see the man slide around the corner of the house, watching him.

It wasn't until fingers curled into his shaggy haircut that he noticed anything out of the ordinary. A hand clamped over his mouth, and he struggled, landing a good kick to the guy's knee, but it didn't do him any good. He picked him up, wrapped an arm tightly around him, and walked out of the yard, closing the gate behind him.

A trunk popped open, and Benny fell inside, rolling and looking up at his kidnapper. A blur surrounds him, just like Dan described. I work to separate the blur from the man. It takes me a minute, but Deleriel's form detaches from the man enough so I can make out his features. He's thin, his face lean and cruel, but his green eyes disturb me the most. They're pure evil. I've never understood what people meant about looking into the face of pure evil, but I do now. I want to run and hide, but I refuse to give in and break the connection. I study him until I have every nuance of his face memorized. He's not going to hurt anyone else after today.

I don't bother looking at Deleriel. It'll only serve to worsen my own anxiety over our meeting tonight. I can't do anything about what has to be done, now that I'm sure I'm right. Seeing Deleriel and his host confirms my suspicions. I'm not walking away from this. What I can do, however, is draw a sketch so detailed, there will be nowhere to hide for this sick pedophile.

I let go of both their hands, and the pain whooshes back like a lightning bolt right to the temple. Freaking hurts. I double over, clutching my head. I see the first drops of blood on my jeans. Swiping at my nose, my fingers come away bloody. This can't be good. At least I didn't pass out.

"Mattie." Dan grabs me by the arms and shakes me. I blink, my eyes coming to rest on him. He looks scared. I can see his own nose dripping blood. No, definitely not good. Silas protected me with his tattoo, but he didn't protect Dan from the side effects he shouldn't be feeling.

"I'm fine." I don't even recognize my voice. It sounds distant, hollow.

"You are not fine, Emma Rose." Zeke grabs my hands when I reach for my sketchbook. "We need to get you back to the hospital. Your nose is bleeding."

"She's okay." Benny pipes in. "Her nose bleeds all the time. Whenever she does her magic, it starts to bleed. Silas told me not to worry. He gave her a tattoo that would keep her from dying."

"He gave you a tattoo?" Zeke starts looking for it.

"On my back, and no, I'm not taking my shirt off. I need to do this before I lose the image. Let me work." I shrug off Zeke and pick up my sketchpad and start to draw.

I block out the sound of them arguing. I focus on the lines and shadows of the image I'm creating. Every detail I remember flows into the page. More people come into the room. I'm barely aware of Benny squealing and jumping into his parents' arms. I can't lose my concentration; I have to do this. His nose isn't quite right. Smudging it a tad brings it back to the reality of the image floating right behind my eyes. His eyes, I save for last. It's harder to get the eyes right. How to show so much evil?

What feels like hours later, I finally look up. The room is quiet, with only Zeke and Dan sitting quietly by his desk. My fingers are cramped, and my eyes burn like I've been awake for days, but the image in front of me could be a digital photo, it's so exact. Right down to the tiny creases along his eyes where the first signs of crow's feet are starting to form. Even I know how good this is, and I usually always find faults with my own work.

"I'm done." Yawning, I flex my fingers, trying to loosen them up.

The sound of my voice startles them both, and they turn, surprised. Dan is the first one up and taking the sketchpad from me. He studies the image, his face completely empty for once. I don't know if that's good or bad.

Zeke takes the drawing from him. "This is…it's…"

"It's disturbing." Dan takes a shaky breath. "But it's brilliant."

"Disturbing?"

"Mattie, you've captured everything I couldn't describe. It's like I'm looking into the eyes of a dead man, a mass murderer…a…"

"Evil." Zeke hands the drawing back to Dan. "She captured the evil of his soul in his eyes. Is this what Silas helped you do?"

I nod slowly. "I learned to look beneath the mask and see what's there. It's habit now."

"You could see that in a vision?" Dan sets the sketchpad down.

"Well, in a way. I couldn't completely see everything, but I saw enough of the madness in his eyes to capture it."

Zeke walks over to the door and opens it, speaking softly.

"I'm guessing he's calling James in."

"They're not gone?"

"No." Dan glances at the drawing. I get the feeling he doesn't want to be in the same room with it. "James wanted it the minute you were done. Plus, Benny refused to leave until he could say goodbye. I think he fell asleep on the couch."

"What time is it?"

"After three, I think."

"He usually falls out about this time." I shake my head. Kids and their schedules. "Wait, did you say after three?" I was working on that thing for three hours? That means I have less time to get everything ready for my meeting with Deleriel. So much to do, and I wasted precious time. This was important, though. It needed to be done so that sickko can't hurt any more children. Deleriel going to ground won't stop the guy from continuing his torture.

"Yeah, Squirt. You tend to lose all track of time when you're in your zone."

True, but still. I hadn't planned on spending that much time on the thing.

Benny bursts through the door ahead of his parents, and Dan quickly snatches the drawing off the table. No need to subject the kid to it. I shoot him a grateful glance as I brace for impact. The kid doesn't disappoint. He hits like the next big linebacker in the NFL and it's all I can do to stay on my feet.

"Hey, there, kiddo." He hugs me tight and buries his head in my stomach. "Well, as much as I love the hug, what's up?" Something is definitely wrong. He's getting as clingy as that first day he woke me up.

"I want to stay here with you."

His bald statement causes his mother to gasp. I can't even imagine what's going through her head. "Why don't you want to go home? Your family missed you."

"You're my family too." He holds on tighter.

"You betcha, kid, but I think you'll hurt you mom's feelings if you don't go home."

"You can protect me from the bad people."

My heart almost shatters at the fear in his voice. I bet he's afraid of going back to the place where he was taken. Being kidnapped is traumatic. I know he has nightmares. Not as many as I do, but he has enough.

I drop down on my knees in front of him. I'm not tall by any means, but I want to look him in the eyes. "There are a lot of bad people in the world, Benjamin. It's not right, but there are. That's why we have people like Dan and your Dad who go out and find the bad people and make them pay for their crimes. They make it safe for the rest of us."

"No one protected me from…him." He wipes the tears out of his eyes. "No one."

My eyes sweep up to his mom. She's shattered.

"I know, baby boy, but that's life. It's hard and not fair, but now you know what to do, who to look out for. It'll be harder for anyone to get the jump on you. You remember everything I taught you, right?" During our stay, I'd taught him how to fight, how to pick a lock, and how to move like the best pickpockets you'll find anywhere. Kid's got skills now.

He nods.

"Then you're prepared. Besides, do you think anyone is getting past Damien? Silas gave you that hound so no one, and

I mean no one, can ever hurt you again."

"He's nice, for a demon." A smile pulls the tips of his lips up. "Even if he is stingy with pudding."

I laugh at how surly he gets over pudding. He and Silas were forever fighting over it. "Now, no more talk of not going home with your mama. She missed you, and I doubt you'll get five inches away from her for the next few years. You have nothing to worry about with so many people looking out for you."

"Promise?"

"Promise." I jump up and ruffle his hair. "Besides, anyone messes with you, and they have me to deal with."

"I love you, Emma Rose."

"I love you too, kiddo."

Heather Malone brushes the tears out of her eyes and comes over to hug me, whispering, "Thank you."

James is next in line. "Caleb told us what you did to save Benny. I won't argue you shouldn't have done it, because it brought me back my boy. Thank you."

"You're welcome." I'm uncomfortable with all the attention and all the thanks, so to deflect, I take the sketchpad from Dan and hand it over to James. "Here. This should help."

James studies the image as intently as Dan had, his teeth worrying his bottom lip. He lets out a low whistle. "This is...it's...it's good."

"I think if you run it through AFIS or even the DMV, you'll get a hit." Dan leans over my shoulder, pointing to the drawing. "I was able to get hits for all the photos she's ever done for me."

"I don't doubt it." His eyes trace the photo with a rage that burns so deep, it's almost impossible to understand. But I do. He wants to hurt the thing that hurt his family. Something I know all too well.

"Benny was never touched, Mr. Malone." I keep my voice down so Benny can't hear. He's playing with Damien and not paying us any attention. "Silas snatched him before any harm came to him. He had some bruises from rolling around in the trunk, but that's all."

"You're sure?" James asks, glancing at his son.

"I'm sure. Benny confirmed it for me."

He lets out a breath I doubt he even knew he'd been holding. "Thank you for everything."

"He's a good kid. Just don't try to separate him from his hound. Damien will make sure no one gets near him again."

James runs a hand through his hair. "A Hell Hound...never did I think we'd have one in the house."

"Benny knows how to take care of him." I give him my best reassuring smile, but I don't think any sane person can ever be reassured about a Hell Hound as a family pet. "Is there anything else you need from me?"

"No, Mattie. You've done more than enough." He hugs me tight, and I can feel the emotions rolling off him, things he'll never be able to express, but they're there all the same. "When you graduate, find me, and I'll give you a job as our team's sketch artist."

"Uh, thanks, but no thanks. I'm not

going anywhere near any kind of law enforcement, thank you very much."

Dan laughs. "You keep telling yourself that. You're going to make a fantastic cop."

"Nope, *Officer Dan*, never happening."

The relief on Zeke's face is comical. I almost choke trying to keep from laughing. I have criminal tendencies of my own. Law enforcement and I have a rocky relationship as it is.

"If that's all, I'm kicking everyone out. I need a shower and some serious sleep. That means you too, Dan. I'm sure Mr. Malone can use all the help he can get right now tracking down your new lead, and I am about to fall flat on my face."

He frowns, about to argue, when I shush him.

"No more protection demons, remember? I'm perfectly safe. I'll even be down here where everyone can watch me."

As much as he doesn't want to leave me alone, the cop in him won't let him walk away from his responsibilities, and that's what I'm counting on.

I need him gone so I can sneak out and get this showdown over with. I'm done putting the people I care about in danger. I have to face this on my own. I don't need anyone to do that.

"Okay, but I'll be back soon, and we'll deal with this whole Deleriel thing, okay?"

"You got it, Officer Dan." I hug him, very aware this may be the last time I ever do this, but I keep my emotions locked down. If he senses anything wrong, there will be no arguing with him. He'll park his butt on the couch and watch me all night.

Once everyone has said goodbye, I sink down on the couch, waiting for my dad to come back in. He looks relieved to have an FBI agent who has actively gone after him in the past out of his home. Not that I blame him. I get twitchy when cops are around too. Too many memories.

"You do not have aspirations of a career in law enforcement, do you, *ma petite*?"

"No." I burst out laughing at the thought. "They'd take one look at my rap sheet and lock me up on principle."

Zeke grins at me. "That's my girl."

Jumping up, I fake yawn. "I need a shower and then some sleep. I really am dead on my feet."

"I'm not sure I want to let you more than five inches away from *me*." He pulls me into a hug. "You scared me."

"I'm fine, Papa. Promise."

He leans back, serious. "I know you are. You're a Crane, and we're always fine, but sometimes we can be not fine, and it's okay."

"I'm glad you found me."

"So am I."

"I love you, Papa."

He nearly stops breathing when I tell him that, and I only hug him in return. "I love you too, Emma Rose Mathilda Hathaway Crane. I love you too."

It's about all I can do to keep my face straight as I excuse myself to grab a shower. That was hard, and I hate what I'm about to do to him.

But it has to be done.

Chapter Twenty-Four

I'm in the shower so long, Zeke sends Mrs. Banks to check on me. He's overly paranoid after the wraith attacked. I did take a little time. I brought my sketchpad up here so I could write a few letters. One to Zeke, one to Dan, one to Mrs. Cross, one to Mary, and finally, one to Eli. My "just in case" scenario. If I don't survive this, I want to be able to tell them all everything I want them to know.

I figured out something. There is no way for Deleriel to get what he wants just by consuming my powers. It won't work like that. I can't draw a doorway for him and leave the intent to let him use it whenever behind. My magic doesn't work like that. He will need a conduit to come and go between the planes, holding and closing the doorway for him. Which would be me.

I'm going to offer to be that conduit for him if he'll let Mary go. I'll make a deal, but I won't tell him what I'm going to do once he uses me as a conduit. The minute he merges with me, I'm going to dismantle him piece by piece. I remember what my mother said. It didn't click until I saw him shadowed over the pedophile in Dan's vision. He was made, and he can be unmade. There's only one slight problem. In order to do that, I'm going to have to do it while his essence is my own, which means I'm going to unravel myself.

It's why I don't want anyone near me to try and stop me. And they will *all* try to stop me, but I figure this is my punishment. I've wrecked all their lives. The least I can do is bring Mary back alive, if not unharmed, and make sure no more kids go missing, as well keep Deleriel away from my family. I will do this for them because I love them.

My unruly mess of hair brushed, I pull on the jeans, t-shirt, and jean jacket Mrs. Banks left on the bed in Dan's room. She knows my style so well because it's like hers. Casual. Nothing fancy. Thank you, Mrs. Banks.

Back downstairs, I make a beeline for the living room and its comfy couch. Not nearly as comfortable as the one in Zeke's office, but still, it's nice enough to get lost in. I plop down and stretch out, laying my phone on the coffee table.

"You're ready for that nap, huh?" Josiah walks into the room, his eyes darting to his phone every five seconds.

"Yeah." Another fake yawn makes Josiah yawn himself. I could never figure out why when one person yawns, it sets off a chain reaction. Odd, but very true. "You guys go ahead and do whatever. All I ask is that you stay quiet, or I will never sleep. I wake up at a whisper."

Josiah quirks a brow. "You used to sleep like the dead when you were a baby."

"Not anymore. I don't sleep well. The

smallest sound sets off alarm bells, and I'm awake."

"Why?"

"A combination of things, from having to learn to protect myself in foster care to what happened to me with Mrs. Olson. I just can't sleep well."

He looks sorry for asking, worried it brought up too many memories. He did, but I'm learning to deal with it.

"We will let you sleep in peace, sweetheart." He comes over and kisses my forehead. "I'll be down the hall if you need anything. Your papa is on the phone with a voodoo priestess we know in New Orleans. Hopefully, we'll know how to bind Deleriel soon without putting you in harm's way."

I smile, but I can't put any real warmth in it. There is no way to bind him. It's a simple truth that I just know. Perhaps it is that small piece of the divine I carry inside, but it's enough to tell me I'm right.

Once Josiah walks out of the room, I close my eyes and pretend to sleep. I'll let him check on me twice, which should give me enough time to establish I'm passed out cold. When they start coming less and less frequently, I can sneak out.

I lie there for a good hour, and it actually feels great to rest. I do need some sleep, but I'm afraid if I catnap, I'll oversleep, and Dan will be back. He can't find me.

Calling for Kane, I stay still, aware my father has just walked into the room. He won't be able to see Kane, who should hopefully pop in soon. Zeke stands beside the couch, staring down at me. I can feel his eyes. I keep my breathing even and steady. He mutters something when his phone chirps and all but runs out of the room. I'm guessing Josiah warned him about me waking up at the drop of a pin.

Anther ten minutes or so tick by, and finally Kane pops in. "You fell asleep?"

"No," I whisper. "I just want everyone to think I'm asleep."

"Why?"

"Because I need to sneak out. Is anyone standing in the hallway?"

I feel his energy move through the

room and come back. It's weird. He has no footsteps, but I can feel him move without even opening my eyes.

"Coast is clear."

Finally. I sit up and quietly go to the front door, letting myself out.

Kane appears instantly as I hit the down button on the elevator. "What's going on, Mattie?"

"I'm going to meet Deleriel."

"You're what?" He's shocked. He'll get over it.

"You heard me."

"Alone?"

"Yup." I hit the ground floor button impatiently. It never makes it go faster, but it makes me feel better.

"Why in God's name would you do that?"

"Because this way, the only person to get hurt will be me. I need your help, Kane. If there's a way to keep Dan alive, I need you to do it."

He shakes his head as the door opens and I'm relieved to see the lobby empty. Good. I slip out the doors and make a beeline for the street. I know where I'm going. There's a church a few streets down that's abandoned. This is going to go down there. They'll think I want to get as far away as I can, and I'm going to use that to my advantage.

"Mattie, that's not going to happen." Kane falls into step beside me. "The two of you are soul-bound. If you die, so does he. No one is going to let him escape death twice. Even if there was something I could do, they'd just undo it."

It's times like these it's hard not to cuss, but I refrain. One of those things I can't bring myself to do.

"Will it be painful?"

"He'll feel everything you do. You've seen it already. Your headaches transferred over to him, and it caused his nose to bleed. He would have had massive brain trauma, same as you."

I close my eyes for a second. *I'm so sorry, Officer Dan.*

"Okay. There goes plan A. On to plan B."

"Plan B?" He flips his hair out of his eyes. "What's plan B?"

"I'm going to reap as many of

Deleriel's children as I can, and I need you to harvest them and ferry them to the other side."

He's completely silent as we walk. I can't even guess what's going through his head.

"Mattie, that's not going to weaken him. His strength isn't tied to the children."

"I know. I just want to ease their suffering. I know exactly how I'm going to deal with Deleriel."

"And?" he prompts when I stop talking.

"And you'll see when we get there."

He grabs me by the arm, pulling me to a stop. "Mattie, what's going through that head of yours?"

I smile and start walking again. He lets me go when he sees I'm not budging. Soon, the church comes into sight, and I glance around to make sure we're alone. No one on the street that I can see. Hopping the fence, I slide around the side of the old stone church. The back is littered with trash, empty beer cans, and needles. A hangout for junkies and those looking for a convenient place to party.

The back door opens easily, the lock having been broken already by the people who vandalized the place. Inside, it's dark. I ask Kane to do that glowy light thing, and we can see within a few seconds. The place stinks, but then it's been empty for over ten years. It should reek of mold and decay. A few of the wooden pews survived the years. Others seem to have been busted up for fires or simply because someone thought it was cool to desecrate a church.

The altar has been defiled. It reeks of urine. Someone tagged the place too. Gang signs. This whole place makes me sad.

"So, what now?"

"Now, we wait. Deleriel knows I'm here."

"Then I'll wait with you."

"No. Go wait with Dan. He needs you more than I do right now."

"Mattie…"

"No. I'm serious, Kane. I don't need anyone to help me. I'm Mattie Freaking Louise Hathaway. Foster kid. I need no one. I survived on my own for years. I don't need anyone to come rescue me. I rescue myself."

"You're an amazing girl, you know that?"

"I do." I give him an impish grin. "Now go be with Dan. And, Kane?"

"Yeah?"

"Not a word about this to him. Promise me."

He purses his lips, but nods. "Not a word about this stupidity of a plan."

When he disappears, I sit gingerly on one of the pews and look up at the massive cross still on the wall behind the preacher's podium.

"Well, God, it looks like I've run out of options. There's no escaping this, so I'm not even going to ask for that. Just take care of my family when I'm gone. Make sure they're okay. I do need something, though. I need strength to do this. I talked a good game with Kane, but I'm terrified. Please, Lord, give me the strength to do what needs to be done."

My digital watch tells me I've sat here for over an hour when a chill creeps over me. The cold sweeps through the room, and I look around, the shadows deep now that Kane took his light away. I can barely see. The cold closes in around me, but it feels different. This feels comforting instead of terrifying like ghosts usually are.

"God can't help you."

His voice is as beautiful as he is. Musical. But cold, colder than the ghosts in the room. Twisting, I see him standing at the back, the glowing yellow eyes of his children all around him. David stands at his side, the one child I want to help more than the others. He still has a spark of his soul in there. I felt it when I spoke to him in the hospital. Somewhere, there's still good in him, and I intend to find it.

"I didn't ask God for help, I asked for strength. There's a difference." How in the world do I sound so calm when I'm shaking in my boots on the inside?

"True." He walks further into the room, the soft halo of light around him bathing the room, allowing me to see for the first time since Kane left. "You surprise me, Ms. Hathaway. I expected to be confronted by your guard as well as whatever your father drummed up."

"Why should it surprise you I'm alone? I've been alone since I was five. I've handled everything thrown at me by myself. I don't need anyone else to fight my battles for me."

"That's charming." He smiles, and David sniffs. He comes closer, right up into my face, and sniffs. "What do you smell, child?"

"Souls." The word is hoarse and drawn out. The kid probably doesn't speak much.

"I reaped some souls that need to be ferried through the Between." Actually, I need the power they give me to pull this off. It's why I hadn't asked Kane to take them. I understand more about reapers than he thinks. Silas and I had several discussions on their oddities.

"You should have given them to your teacher before you came here."

"No time. I sent him to keep Dan and Eli away from here."

"I admire you, girl. Not many would

have the strength of will to face me alone to protect her loved ones."

I don't care if he admires me or not. I just want to get this over with. "I'm here like you asked. Let's get this done."

"You're willing to give me your soul?"

"Not until you bring Mary here and promise to never go after her again."

"Mary is quite content, I assure you."

"That's not the deal, Deleriel. You told me I could exchange my soul for her safety. Bring her here now, or there's no deal."

"It's moot." He flashes a smile at me, one full of teeth. "I don't need you anymore. My children have provided me a means to stay here indefinitely."

Crap on toast. I knew it. He did figure it out.

"Ah, I see you know about my new power source."

"Yes, I killed the one you let loose in the Between."

Something flickers in his eyes, but it's there and gone so fast, I can't describe it. I hit a sore spot, though. I'm sure of that.

"That's impossible."

"Not for me."

"Yes, let's discuss you." He seems to grow taller right before my eyes, and the haunting beauty of his face morphs into something equally as scary. "How do you have a piece of the divine in your eyes?"

"The divine?" I play stupid. Easy to do since I don't want to admit it to myself.

He narrows his eyes, searching my face. I'm the best there is at lying, from my expressions to body language. I have no doubt I look curious and confused. It's what I want him to think.

"Is it possible you don't know?" He's asking himself more than me.

"There are a lot of things I don't know, but I do know we had a deal."

He laughs. "No, girl, we did not have a deal. I gave you an ultimatum, not a deal."

Well, fudgepops, he's right about that. "Let's make a deal, then."

"Why would I do that? I don't need you anymore."

"That's where you're wrong." Lies, all lies, but I have to embrace it right now. "What you want is a permanent doorway.

Yes, eating energy will give you the strength of will to resist being forced back into your prison, but why risk it? What happens when you run out of children? What then? I can give you a permanent doorway."

"How?"

"Even if you were to take my soul from me, you'd never be able to keep a door open. You need someone who can be a conduit, opening and closing the door at will. I can draw you a doorway and instill my will into, but as soon as I die, so does the intent in that drawing. But if you use me as a conduit instead, the door will always be there."

Deleriel stalks over and closes his hand around my throat, lifting me off my feet. Choking, I dig at his hands. "Girl, if you are lying to me…"

"I'm not!" I gasp out. "My magic will die with me. Even if you were to consume my soul, you still need a conduit that is part of the human world and part of the demon realm. I have one foot firmly planted in each. You need my human side to anchor your doorway here on this plane."

Lies, but it's the best I've got.

"You are an exceptionally good liar." He grins at last. "Probably one of the best I've ever seen. You're mixing truth with lies so well, it sounds like the truth, but it doesn't smell like it. Don't you know a demon can smell lies, girl? Did Silas teach you nothing? You are going to speak the truth to me, or I am going to hurt you in ways even Silas can't imagine."

Fudgepops.

The door to the church bursts inward and a blazing white light steps through. Eli Malone, in all his Guardian Angel glory, stands there, the sword in his hand held so tight, I'm surprised he hasn't crushed the hilt.

"Put her down."

The smile grows on Deleriel's face, and he lets me fall, my head bouncing off the pew so hard, I see stars. He leans over me and laughs. "I do believe your Guardian Angel just realized how much he loves you."

What…no!

I look to where Eli is staring at me. The danger he thinks I'm in only enhanced our bond, and his curse thinks he loves me because of how far he's willing to protect me.

"This should be fun." Deleriel steps aside so I'm in full view of one very curse-induced Guardian Angel. I know that look in his eyes. I've seen it so many times before.

Eli Malone just became my executioner.

Chapter Twenty-Five

That soft, gentle smile decorates his face. Those beautiful aqua eyes that have starred in more than a few dreams lazily swirl with nothing but sheer love. This is exactly what Heather had feared and why she ordered Eli to stay away from me, but there is no keeping my Guardian Angel away when I'm in danger.

"You see, girl, I knew all about Silas's plottings. I created my own back door in the form of this curse."

"I saw what you did with Abagail."

"I haven't heard her called that since the day I met her. She was an amazing woman. Sadly, poor Tara was only useful to me so long as she served a purpose. Once that purpose was done, I allowed her death."

I scramble to my feet and put the pews between Eli and myself. He's hopped up on Guardian Angel juice. I don't stand a chance against him when he's like this.

"There is no escaping him." Deleriel chuckles as Eli comes closer. His eyes are zeroed in on me. The front door is behind him, and Deleriel has the back door blocked. I'm stuck, and there is no place to hide in this small room.

Eli walks slowly toward me, that creepy gentle smile on his face I've seen on the men who murdered their wives because of the stupid curse. I slide sideways in the opposite direction. I'm doing my best not to run. I know for a fact running only escalates this whole process. I'm hoping this will slow his insatiable need to murder me.

He cocks his head, studying me. "Why are you running, Hilda?"

"Because I don't want you to kill me."

"I love you, Hilda. I'm protecting you."

"No, you're not, Eli." Another step closer to the front door. "It's the curse. It's making you think that by killing me you're protecting me."

He holds out his hand. "Come here, sweetheart."

"No." My hand brushes up against something, and it burns my fingers. Iron. Glancing down, I see a crowbar. One of those old ones made from iron. It's going to hurt like nobody's business, but it's a weapon. Grasping it, I hiss when my skin starts to blister.

"What are you doing, Hilda?" He surprises me and jumps over the pew, landing a few inches from me. Without thinking about it, I swing the heavy metal bar at him, and it lands squarely against the side of his head. I don't think, I just run. Making it outside the church, I hit the street and run for all I'm worth, praying I didn't hurt him too badly.

He's not himself. I know that. It makes my stomach twist thinking I might have done him serious damage, but I keep running instead of turning back to check on him. I'm not far from the Crosses'.

Zeke picked a location very close by so he could be only a few minutes away.

Years of pickpocketing steer my feet down alleys, letting the shadows hide me. Dan has to be feeling all this panic and fear I can't suppress. I have a freaking Guardian Angel trying to kill me, as well as a Fallen Angel who thinks he doesn't need me. Which leads me back to Mary.

"Silas!"

It only takes the demon a moment to appear, but I run right past him. He catches up within a moment. "Why are we running?"

"Eli's curse decided now is the best time to rear its head," I pant, my legs burning.

"Do you want me to get rid of the boy?"

"What? No! You'll hurt him. I will deal with Eli, but Deleriel is refusing to return Mary. If you want me to kill him, you need to go get my sister."

"You can't kill him."

"Yes, I can." I run up the porch steps unlock the door with the hidey key. "Trust me, Silas, I figured it out.

Someone gave me the answer I needed. He was made, and he can be unmade. But I will not do it until my sister is safe. That's my deal, Silas. Take it or leave it."

"Fine, but I'm not leaving you here alone with no protection against your Guardian Angel." He snaps his fingers, and the hound appears instantly. "Ginger, keep Emma Rose safe. Let no one harm her."

"Tell her not to kill Eli. I won't have him harmed, Silas."

He growls, but does as I ask. "Ginger, do not kill her Guardian Angel, but do not let him harm her." With that, he poofs out.

"Ginger, don't eat me." I twist the deadbolt and run to the kitchen, throwing the crowbar down as I go. My hand is on fire, and I need to run cool water over it.

Deep, heavy knocks vibrate through the house. "Hilda, I know you're in there. You can't run from me. I'll always find you." The sing-song crazy lilt in his voice makes my hackles rise, and I forgo the cool water and grip the large butcher knife instead. I don't want to hurt Eli, but

I won't let him kill me.

Running up the stairs, I go into Mary's room and lock the door. Her window has an escape route. She and I mapped it out when I moved in. Her room has the lowest access point to the roof we can grab onto. We felt safer having one after surviving our capture. Lifting the window, I squirm out of it and use the sill to stand on. Grasping the edge of the slanted roof, I put the knife in my back pocket. This will not end well if I fall, but I need both hands to get to the roof. Then all I have to do is get to the front porch and slide down. We made sure it worked. Mrs. C. about had a stroke when she saw us climbing up and down, but once we explained to her what it was, she stopped arguing. It was therapy for us. We needed it.

And, boy, am I glad we came up with it.

The front door crashes in, and I hop up, or at least try to. My burned hand is being difficult. Why can't it go numb when I need it to?

"Hilda, come out, come out, wherever

you are."

Crap on toast. He's looking around downstairs, thinking I'll want to keep the front door as my main access point. I never told him about the escape route, thank God. Gritting my teeth against the pain, I haul myself up onto the roof.

Wind rips at me, nearly knocking me off the danged thing. I stare at the sky, my voice completely hostile. "Give me a break, here! Do I not have enough to deal with *without* You throwing wind at me too?"

Another loud crash sounds below me. Has to be Mary's door he busted open. The growl that emanates from beneath sends every hair on my head standing up. Ginger. I'd forgotten about her.

"Your watchdog isn't going to stop me from finding you, Hilda." His voice goes deeper, gravelly. He's seriously morphing out into Guardian Angel mode. Silas will murder me himself if Eli kills his hound! Dang it.

"Don't hurt her, Eli!" I shout.

"Then call her off," he shouts right back.

"I can't. Silas ordered her to protect me."

"Her blood's on your hands, then."

"No. I made Silas order her not to kill you. Don't you dare kill that dog!" I wince when I hear the fighting begin. I can't wait here and see what happens. I have to get away from Eli. Running isn't an option up here, I decide when another wave of wind hits and I almost lose my footing. The painful cry of the hound makes me pause halfway over the roof. Silence. *Please don't have killed her. Please.* I take a few more steps, and my foot slides against a loose shingle. Losing my balance, I fall, tumbling down. The chimney stops my roll, but does some serious damage to my side. There will be bruises.

"There you are."

I look up to see Eli standing on the roof line, staring down at me. His face is so peaceful. He's going to kill me. I'm not going to get away from him. The truth of it settles into my heart, and it breaks just a little more. But I refuse to give up. I will fight him to my last breath.

He jumps, and I do my best to stand. I can't roll. Clutching at the chimney, I gain my feet just as he reaches for me. Ducking, I throw caution to the wind and run for the porch. It's only a few feet away, and then I can run. Not sure to where, but anywhere Eli is not.

Not that it means anything. Freaking bond can find me anywhere I go.

Another gust of wind catches me, and I trip, sliding face forward along the downward slope of the roof. I reach out, trying to grasp anything to hold onto, but there isn't anything to grab. The very rapidly approaching ground pulls a scream out of me, but before I can fall, Eli grabs me, twisting so that when we hit the ground, it's his back that takes the brunt of it. It's hard enough to knock the breath out of us both, though.

Wait, he saved me from falling? The curse should have forced him to watch me die, but he didn't. The Guardian Angel bond. It's stronger than the curse. I just have to convince Eli of that. He can fight it. I know he can.

"You are trouble." His hand finds the

knife I stuck in my back pocket, and he pulls it free. No, no, no. Not stabbing. Been there, done that, not doing it again. I kick him hard right between the legs, but he only grunts and flips me over, settling on top of me, the knife in my field of vision.

Flashbacks to the day my mom stabbed me flood my mind, temporarily paralyzing me.

"You shouldn't have run from me, Hilda."

Eli's soft words tear me out of my self-induced panic and right back to his aqua eyes. "You don't have to do this, Eli. You can fight it. I know you can."

"Fight what?" He presses the tip of the knife against my throat.

Police sirens wail in the distance. Someone must have called the cops when they saw us on the roof.

"Please don't do this, Eli, please."

"I have to." He shakes his head, as if to clear it. "I have to, Hilda."

"Why?"

"Because I love you."

Car doors slam, and police order him

to stand down.

"Don't shoot!" His dad. Thank God. "That's my son, don't shoot."

"Eli, you're my Guardian Angel, you're sworn to protect me. If you kill me, you're not protecting me. You're hurting me." I drown out the shouting all around us and focus on him. "Think it about it. Why wouldn't you let me fall off the roof? Because you protect me. That's what you do."

Sweat breaks out across his forehead. He's fighting. I can see it in his eyes. He's fighting. "Think, Eli. This isn't you. It's the curse making you do it. Just stand up and drop the knife. It'll be okay, I promise."

He blinks and jumps up and away from me. "I love you, Hilda."

"I know." I sit up. "Drop the knife, Eli. Please."

"Listen to her, son. Drop the knife." James inches closer, fear written in every line of his body. "You don't want to hurt her."

"But I do, Dad. I can't help it. I can't make this feeling go away. I'm going to hurt her. I can't control it."

"Yes, you can! You just did when you moved away from me."

He shakes his head, blinking rapidly. Guns are trained on him, and I know if he tries to get near me, son of an FBI agent not, they will shoot.

"Please, Eli. Put the knife down." He looks up at me, and the torture in his eyes is too much. The first tears leak out. "Please, Eli. Please."

"I'm sorry I tried to hurt you, Hilda. I'm so sorry for everything." Without any warning, he plunges the knife right into his chest.

"No!" I scream and run for him. He collapses onto the ground, and I fall to my knees beside him, pulling him onto my legs. "Why? Why did you do that?"

"Because I love you, Hilda."

I feel the bond between us break, snap, and wither into nothingness. Pain lashes at me, beats against me in waves I can't fight. No, he doesn't get to do this. I can save him the same way I did Dan. James reaches us, tears on his face.

"I'm not letting you die today, Eli

Malone. Do you hear me?" I'm shouting, but I don't care.

"It's okay, Hilda." He coughs, blood trickling out the side of his mouth. "I am your Guardian Angel, and I'll protect you from everything, including me."

James is screaming for the paramedics, clutching his son's hand to him like a lifeline. "Boy, don't you dare give up. We're getting you to the hospital and you're going to be fine."

"It's okay, Dad." He coughs up more blood.

"No!" I break down, crying. "Don't you dare leave me, Eli. Don't you do it."

"You don't need me anymore."

"Yes, I do." Why is he giving up? "Please, Eli, stay with me."

"Love…you…Hilda."

He coughs again, and the knife moves.

"Where's the ambulance?"

"They're coming, sir."

One of the officers tries to get me to move away, but I slap his hands. "Don't touch me."

"Leave her be," James orders.

I look up and see Kane standing there,

344

his face expressionless. "No, you can't…"

"Mattie, it's his time. He did what he was supposed to do. He has to go."

I shake my head, snot mixing with my tears. Kane knows I'm going to fight him, and he comes over to squat beside me. "Mattie. You can't keep him."

"I kept Dan alive, I can do the same for Eli."

"Who are you talking to?" James asks.

"A reaper." Eli smiles at me, his teeth bloody. "It's time to go, Dad."

"No." James can't do anything but stare at his boy. "You can't go, son."

"Mattie, you can't save Eli the same way you did, Dan." Kane takes my hand and grips it tight. "Your soul is tied to Dan's. The only way to save Eli is to sever your link to Dan. If you do that, Dan will die from the head trauma he should have the first time. Instantly. You are the only thing keeping Dan in this world, but it's up to you. Dan or Eli."

My hands start to shake as grief overwhelms me. There isn't a world I can live in without Dan Richards.

"Please, Kane." The tears mangle my voice. "Please don't take him."

"I have to."

"Hilda."

My head snaps around so fast, I may have done something to the muscles. Eli is gazing up at me. "Don't talk. Save your strength."

"It doesn't hurt anymore. I want you to be happy, Hilda. I was awful to you, and I'm sorry, but I do love you. The bond is gone, and I'm telling you, I love you, and I want you to go out and be happy. Do that for me."

He coughs, and blood spews out. The ambulance screeches to a halt, and paramedics are swarming us, but it's too late. I know it. I lean down and whisper, "I love you too, Elijah Malone."

He smiles, his lips brushing my cheek. He heard me. I only hope he knows I meant it. I do love him.

I'm pushed out of the way, and the paramedics start to work. James is hunched in on himself. I hug him, not sure he'll take comfort from me or not. I am the reason his son is dead. He surprises me by engulfing me in his arms and crying into my hair.

It usually takes three days for the soul to leave the body because it has to understand it's dead and can't hang around. This is a special case. I watch Eli's soul stand up, look down at himself, and then to me. He gives me that infectious grin of his. Kane goes up to him, wiping the grin off his face. They start walking away from us, speaking quietly. The doorway to the other side opens and they walk through, leaving the rest of us in shock and so much pain it's unbearable.

One thing is for sure.

Deleriel is a dead man.

Chapter Twenty-Six

I slip away while the chaos ensues. One of the officers pulls Mr. Malone over to the side, and while they're busy, it's easy. I walk down the block and start back to the church.

Caleb's pickup rolls up alongside me and stops, but I keep walking.

"Mattie, wait!"

Dan. No! "Get of here right now, Daniel Richards." I just lost Eli and I'm not about to watch Dan die.

He pulls me to him. "What's wrong, why are you crying?"

He doesn't know? I peek around him to see Caleb coming over, concern stamped all over his face. Dear God, they don't know. Why didn't they hear it on the police scanner I know Caleb keeps in his truck?

"It's Eli." The broken sound that escapes me is barely understandable.

"Eli?" Caleb runs over and tries to pull me from Dan, who only turns me away from Caleb, shielding me. "What's wrong with Eli?"

"He…he…I…" I just can't. I bury my head in Dan's chest and cry harder.

"Where is he?" Caleb sounds desperate.

"Mary's." It's all I can manage to get out. Caleb takes off at a dead run. It'll be better for him and his dad to be together.

"He's dead, isn't he?" Dan whispers.

I nod. "He wouldn't hurt me, Dan. No matter what that curse did, he wouldn't hurt me." I break down, sobbing, and Dan sits us down right there on the sidewalk and rocks me.

"Shh, Squirt, I got you." He strokes my hair. "I got you."

It's a long time later when I finally stop shaking. "I have to get to the church."

"The church?" The raw pain in Dan's words cuts at me. He lost his brother. He may not have known Eli well, but he was his brother, and that meant something to Dan.

"Deleriel's at the church." I try to stand, but Dan refuses to let me move.

"We need to go to your dad's. Zeke has a plan."

"It won't work."

"You don't even know what it is."

"I know enough to know that Zeke can't kill him, but I can. Now, let me up, Dan. I need to finish this before he can hurt anyone else."

"Mattie…"

"No. I have to do this, Dan. I have to."

"Why?"

"Because this is the only way to protect the people we love. To make Eli's death mean something. I'm not arguing about this, Dan. You go be with your family, and I'll deal with Deleriel."

"You're stupid if you think I'm letting you walk in there alone. You need backup."

"But not you." I shake my head. "You'll distract me, and he'll use you to hurt me."

"Warrior of God, Truth Sword, and all that. I think I can hold my own. You can argue all day, Squirt, but I *am* going."

Dang it. Why does he have to be so stubborn? Haven't I lost enough for one day?

"Come on, Squirt, let's go." He stands, picking me up in the process. "We're going to do this together. Just you and me. If one of us dies, so does the other, so that gives us an edge."

"Put me down, Officer Dan." I wipe at the tears in my eyes, forcing my grief aside. I don't make it go away, exactly, only channel it into sheer determination. Deleriel is going to die.

"Silas!" I shout the instant my feet hit the ground.

"Why are you calling Silas?"

"To see if he has Mary. He went to get her, since Deleriel refused to return her."

After a full ten minutes, I give up. He doesn't have her, or he'd be here. Trying to break her out is dangerous. He told me just how dangerous. Heck, the wards might have killed him, for all I know.

Besides, if I kill Deleriel, I can go get my sister myself. Silas showed me how to get to his home, and I'm betting I will be able to find my way to Deleriel's from there.

"Let's do this."

The walk to the church is short, and as we approach the now closed front entrance, Dan pulls his sword. The metallic sound of the blade leaving the sheath is ominous. It's not a sword I ever want pointed at me. All the lies I've told? Nope, that thing would judge me within a second or two.

The place is quiet when we enter. Deleriel's not here. Probably off feeding from of the souls he murdered. "Deleriel."

I don't shout. I just say his name. He'll hear me and know I'm back.

"Mattie?"

"What?" I squint, trying to make my eyes adjust to the darkness.

"What is that?" He's pointing to the side, and I turn that way. Dozens of yellow eyes are blinking at us. Crap. He's not here, but he left his children behind.

"Those are Deleriel's kids." Dan has only seen one. I doubt he even knows how dangerous they are.

"This isn't good, is it?"

"No." They shuffle forward, their eyes glowing with need and hunger. They'll devour us before we have time to defend ourselves. "Do you know how to use that thing?"

"No, but that doesn't mean I won't try." He holds the sword out in front of him and steps forward.

The children don't hesitate, they swarm him. And then something happens. Dan seems to grow in height, and he swings outward, the sword plowing through the first wave. They fall, but they don't stay down.

No!

"Stop, Dan, don't kill them!"

The kids who fell pull themselves up into a crouch, the glow gone from their eyes. Dead souls. We just created giant batteries for Deleriel. They spring at me, and I jump out of the way, staring after them as they escape the church.

"Mattie, I don't know what else to do!" He's batting at them, but there are too many. If he doesn't kill them, they'll destroy him.

Think, Hathaway, think.

The only thing I can try is my reaping ability. I close my eyes and concentrate on every memory I have that is full of love and kindness and open the door to the other side. It's a bright golden light, and the children pause and turn toward it. These souls aren't dead, just abused.

"Why did they stop?" Dan whispers.

"Shhh." I walk forward, my hands held out so they can see I don't mean them harm. "Do you see the light little ones? It's nice there. No one can hurt you ever again in that light. Not even Deleriel. It's safe and warm, and people you love will be there. All you have to do is walk into it. It's okay. I promise."

They stare from the light to me, unsure.

"What light?" Dan inches closer to me, and I take his hand so he can see. The hiss of his shock echoes through the room. "That is beautiful."

"Yes, it is beautiful. It's all that is good, children. No more pain. You'll never be hungry in the light. All you have to do is trust me and go into the light."

"The light is dangerous." The snake-like hiss from behind me startles me and I whirl. David is standing there, and the children all freeze, afraid of him. He's their wrangler, their brother, and their warden.

"It's not, David. It's full of joy and love. Your family is there."

"My family?"

I nod and get down on my knees in front of him. Taking his face in my hands, I ignore the evil that surrounds him and focus instead on that small grain of hope that lives in his soul. I reach out and wrap my own reaping power around it, bathing it in as much love and understanding as I can. He whimpers, and the sound breaks my heart.

"Your family, David. Your mom and your dad."

"My brother too?" He cocks his head questioningly, but I can feel his lie. He doesn't have a brother.

"If you had a brother, then yes, he'd be there."

"Father says the light hurts, it will incinerate us."

"He's a Fallen Angel. He lies." I look away from him and back to the others. "He's a liar. The light won't hurt you. It'll heal you."

Dan settles behind me while I try to convince these demonic little monsters to go into the light. It's the only way to save us, but more importantly, it'll save them.

"Trust me, David. That light is your way out. Go, sweetheart. Run to your family and be happy. Just go, little one. Go now." I kiss his forehead, and he jerks back. His fingers graze the place my lips were. He stares at me, his eyes unfathomable.

"It won't hurt?"

"No, it won't."

He nods and turns to face the light. His entire body shakes, but he makes his feet move until he's standing right in front of the light. "Mommy?" This look of sheer happiness replaces the haunted to look on his face. I can see rivulets of black sludge start to fall away from him until more and more of his soul shines. He reaches out a hand and steps forward, the golden light swallowing him.

"You see, children. It's safe. David found his mommy. Your family is there. Go into the light."

They look at each other then swarm the light much the same way they had Dan. The light fades and goes away when the last one disappears into it. Peace. For the first time all day, I feel at peace.

"You're going to pay for that."

Deleriel. A very pissed off Deleriel. His amber eyes glow with an unholy light. He storms toward us, and Dan's sword comes up, which only makes him laugh.

"You think that thing can hurt me?"

"Maybe." Dan's voice has gone deep, and he looks a little fear-inspiring himself.

"I've already caused you to kill your Guardian Angel, girl. Do you want me to hurt your soul-bound warrior as well?"

"No. I don't want anyone else to die." I

stand up and face the Angel. "There's been enough death for one day. I want to make you a deal."

"Mary will be part of no deals. She's mine."

The feral look makes me want to cringe, but I keep my face calm and neutral.

"Fine. I will be your conduit if you leave the rest of my family alone, and that includes the Malones."

He scoffs. "Are we back to that lie again?"

"You've told so many lies, you can't recognize the truth of what I'm saying. You can take my soul, but it will not anchor you to the physical world. A metaphysical link will not do it. You need flesh and blood to stay here. Think about it. When you're here now, you have to body jump people. Do you think that's going to change once you gain my ability? My gift only works because I'm part human, tied to the physical world. Kill me, and that doorway slams shut forever."

"What you say makes sense, girl, but I

still sense deception in you."

"I'm a liar, Deleriel. It's what I do, but this? I'm protecting my family. I'm making a deal with you, and you know what happens when someone breaks their word. They die, and there is no way I will ever willingly do that, because if I die, so does Dan."

Deleriel has a poker face and a half. I have no idea what he's thinking, but for this to work, he has to pass through me.

"I have but one addendum to the contract."

"Which is?"

"You will come with me and remain in my own lair in the deepest corner of Hell. You keep saying you want to see your sister. That is where you'll find her."

"Agreed. Do we have a deal?"

"Mattie…"

"Stay out of this, Dan. It's my deal to make. If it keeps you and everyone else safe, it's worth it." I mouth silently to him, *trust me*.

"We have a deal." The Fallen Angel extends his hand to me, and I take it. The world swirls, and we're falling. The next instant, I'm surrounded by the stench of sulphur.

"Welcome to my home, little reaper." Deleriel smiles, but it doesn't reach his eyes. "Would you like to see your sister before we begin building this doorway to bridge the planes?"

"Yes." If Silas hasn't already sprung her.

He leads me down a hallway to a locked door at the end. He knocks before unlocking it. "Mary, someone is here to see you."

Mary is sitting on a lounge chair, her feet tucked under her and a book in her hand. Her blonde hair spills around her like a halo. She looks up, and her face freezes in the most comical expression I've ever seen. "Mattie?"

I launch myself at her much like Benny does and almost topple us both to the floor. "You're okay. God, Mary, I've been so worried."

"I can't believe you're here." She hugs me so tight I can't breathe. "I didn't think I'd ever see you again."

"How long?" I ask her. "How long

have you been here?"

"A year."

"I'm so sorry." I lean closer to her and whisper so low, there is no way Deleriel can hear me. "We're getting out."

Mary, being astute, doesn't give me away. She just hugs me.

"Enough." Deleriel saunters toward us. "You can speak later. First, little reaper, you are going to build this door and show me how it works."

"Of course." I pull away from my sister and turn around. "A deal's a deal."

Only this deal won't turn out the way he thinks.

Chapter Twenty-Seven

Deleriel locks Mary's door and leads me down a maze of hallways until we come to a room made of stone with dirt floors. Old gas lamps line the walls, giving off enough light to see. A worn desk sits in one corner, and the rest of the space is barren. I'm not exactly sure what the room is for.

"I need a bowl and something to draw with."

He nods and goes to a shelf that magically appears along one wall. Why can't I make things appear? I am half demon. It should be a thing.

He brings back a stone bowl and a

paintbrush. Usually, I'd ask for a charcoal pencil, but for this, it doesn't have to be fancy. Just a plain door.

Holding out my arm to him, I give him the instructions that are going to help me dismantle him. "I have to bind me as your conduit, and you to the door. I need both our blood in the bowl."

He eyes me suspiciously, but quickly slices my wrist and does the same to himself. Power, greed, pride. They vibrate through him. I can smell it.

Once enough of our blood has fallen into the bowl, I swirl it together with the paintbrush, mixing it thoroughly. I use the paintbrush to outline a simple door, with a doorknob. I push my intent into it, making the door that will open and close only for Deleriel whenever he wishes to return to the plane of the living. On my world. The energy snaps into place, our blood serving to cement the door. The outline shimmers and then takes on the look and feel of a real door until what's left is a dark mahogany door waiting to be opened.

Deleriel wastes no time doing just that.

He lets out a delighted chuckle. Before us is Freedom Park in downtown Charlotte. I knew it would work, but in order for him to enter, his essence has to pass through me. That's the catch. I keep myself still when he tries to pass through and the door throws him back.

"What…"

"Don't freak out. I told you, I'm the conduit. In order for this to work, you have to pass through me, the same as you did with your other host. Only you will not have to stay inside of me. You'll be free to roam in a corporeal form, thanks to me as your conduit. One foot in both places, remember?"

"I did not think…" He breaks off, staring me down, but this is a game I'm good at. I stare back, bored. "Fine. But next time you make a deal, girl, make sure you outline everything it entails."

"Noted." I crack my knuckles. "Is this going to hurt?"

"Yes." He smiles and dissolves into smoke. It swirls around me, and I flinch. I do not want him to touch me, but it's necessary. What I do not expect is the body jump. A wail echoes in my ears, and then all that black smoke is pouring down my throat, and he did not lie. It hurts.

Staggering, I work to stay conscious. He's there. I feel every dark pulse of evil as he seeks to leave me and enter through the door. Oh, no, you don't.

I lash out my own light and wrap it around him, binding him with the darkness that lives in me, my demonic side. It's the other side that causes him to scream. I know what he sees. I can see it reflected back at me because we're linked. My eyes have turned to pools of gold with traces of black floating in them. My mother's eyes.

No, you can't.

I can, and I am.

Our deal...

Was to create a doorway in which I would be a conduit. I kept my word. I just didn't tell you what I was going to do once you body jumped me. You're done, Deleriel. For good.

Finding his core, I start to shred it, aware that his is tied to mine. Once he's gone, Silas will find Mary. The sharp rock bites at my hands as I work to pull apart each thread that holds Deleriel together. It's so easy to do. The pain is nothing. This man has caused so many to suffer. The souls inside of me reach out, adding their strength to mine. They wish him gone as much as I do.

He's fighting me, though. Holding him isn't easy. He's more powerful than anything I've ever faced, but I buckle down and reach out for strength, the only thing I prayed for, and it flows into every fiber of my being. Deleriel is not getting away.

The darkness in him flees from my wrath, and his screams assault my ears. Still, I press on, falling to my knees as my legs give out. I keep taking him apart until I'm down to only one small molecule. It pulses with a different light. A holy light. I hesitate. This is the part of him that was an Angel.

A sense of peace settles in my bones, and I know what I have to do. I smash it, and my own scream echoes around me as I smash his soul and my own. Tumbling,

I lie there on the cold dirt floor, spent and in pain.

Not dead, though. Dying, but not dead. I call out for Silas, and I hope he can find my voice. Now that Deleriel is gone, his wards should be gone too. True to my logic, he pops into existence a few feet from me. His eyes widen when he sees me. "Emma Rose…"

"Mary," I whisper, my voice so low it's barely there. "Mary…locked door…get her out."

"Not until I take you to your father."

"Too late. I smashed my soul to kill Deleriel. Please, Silas, take my sister home. Please. I did what you wanted. I killed him. Now honor our deal and take her home." He can't not do it, and he knows it.

"I'll be back for you."

He poofs away, and I giggle. I love that he poofs like the fairies in *Fairly OddParents*. I feel floaty. Maybe I'll become a fairy and just poof away to wherever I want. More giggles spill out, and I close my eyes. It feels like I'm flying.

Am I flying? It feels like the world is moving. I open my eyes and sure enough, everything *is* moving.

"You stupid girl."

No, not flying. Silas is carrying me.

"I told you, warned you…" He cuts off, and then we're falling.

"Silas?"

Zeke. My papa. I wish I could have gotten to know him. I need to tell him how much I love him. Struggling, I open my eyes, but it's not Zeke I see. It's my…

"Mom?"

Claire Hathaway is smiling, her face relaxed. She walks over to me and kisses me. *"My sweet girl."*

"Mama." Tears choke me, and I try to reach out to her. Love and hope surge up, washing away the debilitating pain. My mom came for me.

"Hush, baby. You'll make it worse. I'm here. I've always been here, watching you. Mama is so proud of you, baby girl."

"What's wrong with her?"

"She's dying. The fool girl smashed

her own soul to kill Deleriel."

"I had to, Mama. I couldn't let him hurt anyone else."

"I know, baby." She strokes my hair. *"Be still. It's going to be all right. I promise."*

The same words I'd told the children back at the church with Dan…Dan. "Dan."

"Is fine. Kane is with him. He's not alone."

"Why does she keep saying Mama?" Zeke is more than distraught. He's afraid.

"My guess is her mother came to ease her passing." Silas still hasn't put me down. "But she's not going anywhere, not today. We have a deal, my darling girl. You owe me a favor, and you cannot pass on without fulfilling that bargain."

I can't do anything else. My head lolls backward. "Tired."

"Emma Rose, I demand my favor of you. You will not die this day. You will hold on and fight. Reach out to Dan, that's all you have to do. Find him, and you'll be whole. I swear it."

"The painter is right, my sweet girl.

Dan's soul is whole, and yours, while scattered in pieces, is still attached to him. Just find him, baby, and you'll get better. Mama's here to save you, not to take you. Find him, and I'll help you."

The sound of the ocean waves crashing against the sound fills my senses. Mom and I used to go to the beach and sit on the sand at night, listening to this very thing. It calms me, but I don't have any strength left to reach out to Dan. I'm so tired.

"You're a demon, girl. That's all the strength you need. Deals cannot be broken." Silas's voice floats to me over the sound of the waves.

Our word is our bond. I open myself up, and the darkness rushes in, gleeful and full of bad things, but it does give me strength. At least enough to follow the shining cord that stretches between me and Dan. He's still at the church, lying on the floor. Kane sits beside him, talking quietly. Trying to assure him that I'm okay, and he shouldn't be afraid. Once I'm gone, all the pain will stop, and he can see me soon.

Dan can't die. I won't let him. I worked too hard to steal him away from death. I float toward him, settling inside his soul, my own gone, and it feels so warm. So loved and cherished. He lets out a groan. I hope I didn't hurt him.

"There's Mama's girl." She strokes my hair while I'm still in Silas's arms, but I can feel it here, where I'm nestled in the warmth and safety of Dan's soul. *"Mama is going to fix you now, baby. Just stay still for me."*

I'm not moving. This is where I'm supposed to be. Dan is my home and always will be. No matter what happens, he's mine.

I yawn. Dan's body bucks, and the sleepiness vanishes. What's wrong? Am I hurting him?

"Shhh, baby, just hold still."

My Mama soothes me, and I settle back down, feeling better. I close my eyes and fall asleep, content, wrapped in Dan's soul and my Mama stroking my hair.

***

The steady beeping of machines wakes me up. It's a sound I know all too well. My eyes are heavy and don't want to open, but as the last twenty-four hours crash into me, I struggle to sit up and open my eyes to verify I'm not dead.

How? How is this possible? I smashed my own soul to smithereens. I should be dead.

Looking across from me, I see Dan still sound asleep in the bed opposite me. Our beds are pushed right up against each other. Zeke, I'm betting.

Memories keep flooding in, and the one I latch onto is my mama. She was there, right there beside me. A sob catches in my throat. She came to save me.

"Don't cry, sweet girl." My breath catches. She's standing right beside me and places a hand against my cheek. *"Don't cry. You're safe now."*

"I thought you crossed over."

"I did, but there isn't a force in this universe that could keep me away from

you when you need me."

"How, though? How am I alive? I shattered my soul."

"I went out and found all those pieces floating around and put them back together again."

"Like Humpty Dumpty."

She laughs. *"You did love that rhyme. You'd go around singing it all day."*

"You saved me."

"Of course, I did. I'm your Mama. It's my job to protect you. It's what I've always done. Even when I tried to kill you, it was only to keep you safe. It was the only way I knew how."

"I miss you, Mama. I was so mad for so long, but I miss you."

"I miss you too, baby, Every day." She leans down and kisses me, and I feel it all the way through my soul.

Another thought rears its ugly head. "Kane said as soon as I got rid of Deleriel, his bosses were going to get rid of me."

"It's taken care of." She sits beside me. *"You're safe, baby."*

"But how?"

"Your mother. She stopped it."

"My mother?" What is she going on about? My head is too fuzzy for this.

Another form sorta fizzles into existence. The woman from the Between.

"Mattie, this is Rhea, your mother. She made sure you're safe from those who wish you harm."

"I will obliterate them." The haughtiness in her voice is too much. I don't want the deity here. I only want my mama.

"Sweetheart, I have to go soon, but Rhea is here, and she's just a breath away from you."

"I don't want her, I want you." That five-year-old little girl who never really grew up comes out. "Please, Mommy, stay with me. Please."

"I can't, baby. My time on this earth has passed. I need to go, but I'm not leaving you. I'm always watching, and I know you'll be safe with Rhea." She kisses me again. *"I have to go, baby girl."*

"No, please."

A single tear rolls down her cheek. *"I*

have to. I love you, Mattie Louise. Mama will always love you." With that, she fades, leaving me alone with the mother I don't want.

"Rose. I know it's hard, but I hope you'll give me a chance."

I can't, I just can't. Rolling over onto my side, I don't try to hold back the tears. I cry for Eli, I cry for every lost soul Deleriel destroyed, and I cry for my mama.

"I'm sorry." Rhea touches my shoulder, and I flinch.

"Go away."

"Is there anything I can do for you, Rose?" She sounds as lost as I feel right now.

I start to say no, but there is one thing she can do.

"Can you make me normal? Take all this away and just make me normal?"

"You're not normal, Rose. You never will be. I can't take away what you were born with, but I can put it to sleep. Your gifts will always be there, ready to awaken when you need them. That much I can do."

"Then do it. I don't want it."

"All of it?"

No, not all of it. As much as I want to say yes, I can't. Not after everything I've been through. "Not my reaping ability. I need to see the ghosts, to help them. Everything else, make it go away, Please."

"As you wish, my child." She lays her hand on my head, and a warmth rushes through me from the crown of my head to the tips of my toes. "There. Everything but your reaping ability is asleep. I did leave you the ability to travel planes. I think you promised the demon to visit him."

I'd forgotten that.

"Thank you."

"I'm here when you're ready, my Rose." She leans down and kisses my temple. As soon as she does, she's gone. The room feels emptier than it was.

Dan's hand finds mine, and I look up, meeting those puppy dog eyes of his.

"We got to stop meeting like this, Squirt." He gives me a half smile. "You okay?"

"No."

"You will be, though. You always are."

I'm not so sure.

"You hear all that?"

"Yeah, I'm used to you talking to people I can't see. You gave up all your gifts? Why?"

"Because I'm tired of being a freak show. I just want to go back to my normal. Ghost Girl, remember?"

"Yeah, I remember her. She's kinda cute. Brash, bossy, but cute."

"Shut up."

He laughs and winces. "I feel like I got hit by a Mack truck."

"Me too."

"But it's fine, as long as we're both here."

"In it for the long haul?"

"Yup."

And that is that.

Epilogue

Our plane to New Orleans should be boarding soon. Dan is coming down long enough to get me settled. Right now, he needs to be close to me for a few weeks. My soul is still healing, and it needs his to do that. He can't stay, though. He has to get back for the Malones and for his mom's trial. His dad moved out of the house when he discovered Mrs. R. sent a demon to kill me. It was the straw that broke the proverbial camel's back. If Dan didn't have to be the glue that's holding my soul together, you couldn't pry him away from his family. They're all hurting, the Richards' and the Malones.

Eli's funeral was last week. I asked to be a pallbearer, and much to my astonishment, the Malones agreed. Not that any of them can look me in the eye, but they didn't try to stop me from going or for doing right by Eli. I don't know if this pain will ever heal. He protected me with everything he had. He gave his life for mine. It's a debt I can never repay.

Mary is coming with us. She's so quiet now. Not like the bubbling girl she was, but Zeke is confident she'll recover. I don't know what happened during the year she was trapped with Deleriel. She refuses to talk about it. Zeke knows a counselor who deals with paranormal trauma, as he put it. Hopefully, they'll be able to help her. Her mom understood Mary's need to escape Charlotte and didn't put up a fight when she said she was going with me. She actually threatened my father about what she would do if he didn't keep their girls safe. It unsettled him. There is no fury like that of an enraged mother.

Zeke and I had a long talk about everything that happened. He agreed with my decision to put my gifts to sleep. I need time to heal from all of this before I worry about much of anything else. There will always be time to deal with those pieces that can cause the most trouble.

Silas is going to be a part of my life from now on. I think Zeke has no idea what to say about my grandfather. Silas kept me alive. Zeke told me the demon stood there crying, refusing to let anyone else take me, demanding I live. It startled them all. For all his bluster, he loves me. I really am his favorite. Does that mean he won't hurt me? Nope. Just that he's less likely to cause me permanent damage.

He gave me one of his pups. Her name is Peaches, even though she's black as night. The hound is tiny, the runt of the litter. She's blooded, and I love her. She acts just like a regular puppy instead of a Hell Hound. I'm going to do my best to keep her that way. Silas is keeping her while we're on the plane. You can't very well take an invisible dog on board. He'll drop her off when I get to Zeke's home.

Kane was able to rescue all the souls Deleriel had been feeding on for centuries. Some of them were well past salvageable and I didn't want to know what he did with those. Silas collected one soul out of the lot. His sister, I'm thinking. At least her torment ended. Silas should let Kane cross her to the other side, but I understand his desire to hold her close for a little while. He did say, he was what he was because of his sister. He deserves a little time with her because of everything he did to rescue her. I'll start pestering him in a few months to let me send her on to where she's supposed to be.

Doc called me a few days after everything went down, apologizing that he wasn't there. He had a family emergency and I assured him it was fine. Family comes first. It's a simple truth I hold dear. I can't fault him for bailing on me to take care of his family. I did promise we'd sit down and talk about everything once things have settled down. Dan is happy about that much at least. Maybe he's right. Doc only ever tried to help me. Either way, I owe him a chat.

Boarding for our flight is called, and Dan sidles up. "You ready for this?"

He knows how terrified I am of flying. He actually laughed at me, saying after everything I've survived, I'm afraid of a plane ride. Well, I am. Does he not realize how easy it would be for anything to happen? Then we'd be falling through the air, burning, twisting metal, people screaming…I shudder at the thought.

"Nope. I'm going to sleep as soon as we buckle the seatbelts."

"It's going to be fine, Squirt."

"I know."

And I did. As I hand my boarding pass over, I know deep down I will be fine. We all will. We have to heal, and God knows we need boatloads of therapy, but we *will* be fine.

As long as we're together, we'll be fine.

New Orleans, here we come.

The End

Coming 2018 - *The Crane Diaries*. Follow Mattie's adventures in New Orleans.

Acknowledgements

How do you even go about thanking everyone that made a series so special?

No clue. So I'm going to do my best and hope that anyone I leave out by accident understands they are just as much appreciated as anyone else. Sorry in advance to those I'm sure to forget.

The Ghost Files spanned five years of my life with six books and a novella. It took up so much of my time, my other series got benched for a long time, but I wouldn't have it any other way. Mattie is special to me and to so many others.

A lot of people ask how did I get the idea for The Ghost Files. Well, I was doing dishes in the sink and the curtains above the sink started to flutter wildly. The AC was off and the doors and windows closed. No way could there have been a breeze. My first thought was ghost! Then my brain says, no, there's no such thing as ghosts...but what if there was? The idea took root and the concept was born.

I had met some foster kids previously who it took me almost a year to get to know them. When they started opening up about some of the homes they'd been in, my heart broke listening to their stories. These kids had seen everything from apathy to mistreatment in the form of beatings, starvation, and being locked in dark places. Listening to these kids describe some of the worst places they'd been and survived completely broke my heart.

The home they were currently in was a good one. I knew their foster mother and she spoke with me at great length about the system. It's a horrible, broken system with fail safes that are ignored not out of malice, but because there is no time. There are too many kids assigned to workers and the ball gets dropped because those workers have to prioritize their worst cases against others. Sometimes those others are wolf in sheep's clothing. Kids are too afraid to tell and as long as the place is clean and stocked with food, most social workers will consider it a good home. When it's really not.

The only way this system will get fixed is through people speaking out. If you know that children are being mistreated, speak out, bring all that ugliness to the light of day. Tell anyone who will listen – a teacher, police officer, someone. Nothing will change unless people take a stand and speak out. Get the system the money it needs to hire more workers so they aren't overwhelmed.

Now that my soap box is done, on with the thanking.

First I want to thank everyone at The Next Big Writer where I workshopped the first book. The people on that site are writers themselves and will viciously tear your hard work to shreds, but they do it because they want your words to be the best they can be. Sometimes their criticism put me in near tears, but I took it and worked to correct my missteps. What I got was a stronger book and I'm grateful. You have to have thick skin on that site, but the people there will make you a better writer. So thank you everyone there – especially Lawrence and

Maggie for all your hard work.

Maggie Banks – you tirelessly helped me go through volumes 1-3 and rework what didn't work. Your advice was valuable and I will forever appreciate all that you did. Thank you so very much.

My girls, all amazing authors themselves—Delsheree Gladden, Susan Stec, and Angela Fristoe. You all read the book(s) again and again, helping me when I was stuck, finding creative ways to get me out of the corners I wrote myself into, and just being the cheerleaders I needed when I wanted to quit. I would be nowhere without you three and I want you to know how much that means to me. Thank you three from the bottom of my heart.

Editors are what make an author's work shine. I went through several until I found one that I truly love – Mrs. Lori Whitwam. She taught me how to be a better writer, how to make my words stronger and more meaningful. She taught me less really is sometimes more and how to use actions instead of dialog tags to get my meaning across. It changed the way I wrote and I think for the better. At least readers seem to like it ☺ You are a doll and I refuse to work with any other editor after you have spoiled me with all your dedication and willingness to answer my questions any time day or night. Thank you, Lori, for all you've done for me.

Jennifer O'Neill. When I first started querying this story, I went the agent route and they all turned me down, sometimes in hurtful ways that made me want to quit writing altogether, but you and your small press, Limitless Publishing, took a chance on me when others refused. That means a lot to me and it's why I stick with you today. You believed in me when no one else did. Thank you so very, very much.

Wattpad. From the folks at Wattpad HQ to the readers, you all have done so much for this series. I almost deleted the book, but put it up on the site instead on the advice of a friend. The response was huge and it validated that the book wasn't worthless. Readers loved it and they went out and bought the book even after being able to read it for free on Wattpad. The Watty readers are loyal to a fault and I love them. I wouldn't be here writing the acknowledgements for the end of the series without you guys. As for Wattpad HQ – Caitlin O'Hanlin in particular. You were instrumental in helping me, answering questions and just being supportive. Thank you and everyone else at Wattpad HQ. You make being a part of the community that much more special.

My readers. How can I ever thank you all enough for all the support you've given me over the years? You are why I continued Mattie's story and why I still write today. You are my Knights In Shining Armor. Thank you, thank you, thank you.

Rami Rank and Sharyn Steele. As many of you know, The Ghost Files was optioned for film. Rami Rank is the producer who optioned it. He was the one producer who took the time to answer all my questions, even stupid ones, and explain things to me in terms a layman could understand. There is almost nothing on the internet about options and it meant a lot he took the time to answer everything in full until I was satisfied. He believed in the book as much as I do and that's why I gave him the rights. Sharyn came on board the project later, but is just as important. She believed in Mattie as much as Rami and I did. She worked tirelessly to get it in front of all the right people. I'm so grateful to them both for all the hard work they have put into this project.

The big questions I get all the time…will there be a Ghost Files movie? I hope so. The fans deserve one. And that's really all I can say on the matter ☺

My friends and family what can I really say? You guys know how I get when I'm writing. I go into my hermit-like habits as Chazz will tell me. Unlike everyone else who leaves me alone until I'm done, she refuses to and will pester me until I yell, what??? God bless her. She keeps me out of my own head when I get lost into it and the world I'm writing. She keeps me sane. Everyone else, I hope you know how grateful I am for your support and knowing I miss out on things because this is important to me. Thank you all.

This series has touched my heart and the hearts of others so much. It's hard to say goodbye to characters we love, at least for this chapter of their lives. I'm excited to get started on the new adventures of Emma Rose Crane and her exploits in New Orleans. I hope you'll all join me early next year for the first chapter of her new life.

About the Author

So who am I? Well, I'm the crazy girl with an imagination that never shuts up. I LOVE scary movies. My friends laugh at me when I scare myself watching them and tell me to stop watching them, but who doesn't love to get scared? I grew up in a small town nestled in the southern mountains of West Virginia where I spent days roaming around in the woods, climbing trees, and causing general mayhem. Nights I would stay up reading Nancy Drew by flashlight under the covers until my parents yelled at me to go to sleep.

Growing up in a small town, I learned a lot of values and morals, I also learned parents have spies everywhere and there's always someone to tell your mama you were seen kissing a particular boy on a particular day just a little too long. So when you get grounded, what is there left to do? Read! My Aunt Jo gave me my first real romance novel. It was a romance titled "Lord Margrave's

Deception." I remember it fondly. But I also learned I had a deep and abiding love of mysteries and anything paranormal. As I grew up, I started to write just that and would entertain my friends with stories featuring them as main characters.

Now, I live in Huntersville, NC where I entertain my niece and nephew and watch the cats get teased by the birds and laugh myself silly when they swoop down and then dive back up just out of reach. The cats start yelling something fierce…lol.

I love books, I love writing books, and I love entertaining people with my silly stories.

Facebook:
https://www.facebook.com/authorAprylBaker

Twitter:
https://twitter.com/AprylBaker

Wattpad:
http://www.wattpad.com/user/AprylBaker7

Website:
http://www.aprylbaker.com/

Newsletter:
http://www.subscribepage.com/n0d6y8

BookBub:
https://www.bookbub.com/authors/apryl-baker

Made in the USA
Columbia, SC
25 September 2021